False Reality

David Ruffin

Copyright Page

False Reality © Copyright 2021 By David Ruffin

ISBN: 9798767010059

For more information,
E-mail 4224ruffinbooks@gmail.com

Thank You

To my beautiful and lovely wife Mrs. Jazzįį Ruffin-
I thank Allah (Most-High), every day for bringing you into
my life and heart. If it wasn't for you pushing me every day
the world wouldn't know about my creative mind "False
Reality." I know I get on your last nerve sometimes lol... I
truly love you!

Special super thanks to Ayanna (Thanxamills) Ambrose, for
helping me get my book out to the world and connecting me
with the right editor team... Thanks to Samuel Linda, fixing
all High Maintenance Publishing and Production Company
on purposes mistake.

Dedication

I dedicate this book to my beautiful people worldwide...

To the guard of the Lee County Jail in the 90's, that told me to write down every crazy thought, weird thought, and every dream to start my books.

To my Muslim brother who encouraged me and pushed me to share my books with the world...

To my sons, I love each and every one of you...

To the three beautiful queens of my life; my wife, my mother, and my daughter, you are what inspired and motivated me to bless the world with my wonderful mind as well as FALSE REALITY.

This is only the beginning…

Table of Contents

Chapter 1

My name is Neiros Simmons, some people call me Jizzle, some people call me Death... Shit! Bitches call me a lot of shit, but that's on some other shit. Now y'all bout to come into my world. That shit might sound boring as fuck, or lame as fuck, just trust me, my world is far from boring. Case in point, as of this moment, I got one of my targets in sight. Yeah, one stupid muthafucka that owes some Columbians about fifty 6's. and for some reason, he thinks his ass is untouchable just because he's the Chief of Police. Shiiitt...ain't nobody safe from Death! Nobody! Now, this muthafucka thinks a nigga can't slide up on his ass but peep this shit...

"Umm... Excuse me, Sir... Would you happen to know the time? My watch just stopped working and I need to call the wife, because she's about to go to work" Death said, with a friendly grin, standing 5'11", with a clean-shaven baldhead that shines when the sun hits it.

The Chief of Police hesitated a moment, as he turned around looking at Death in his brown eyes, while taking in his chocolate skin attached to an athletic build, inside his expensive black Armani suit.

"Why... Yes sir... It's 12:20."

"Whew!", Death wipes his forehead with the back of his hand... "Thank you, Sir!" He said, pulling out his cell phone, only to find the battery is dead, "Aw Man!" he exasperates, "Today just isn't my day! Um, excuse me, Sir!"

"Yes," The Chief turns around.

"I don't mean to be a burden, but my phone is dead, so is my car and I really need to reach my wife before she leaves. Would it be possible to use your phone?"

"Actually son, I'm busy, but if you don't mind coming inside...you can use the phone."

"Thank you" answers Death, as they walk towards the house.

On the way to the door, Death does a sweep of the neighborhood, and just as he figured, not a cracked blind was in sight.

As soon as the Police Chief opened the door and stepped inside, Death hit him with a solid overhand punch to the back of the neck, right where the spine starts.

Before he could react, Death completes a swift low inside crescent sweep to the back of his knee, all the while putting the man in a chokehold. Applying just enough pressure to make him pass out.

Two hours later, the Chief awakes and finds himself tied to a chair, with his wife and son sitting in front of him. Panicking, he immediately starts to call out to his wife, begging her to respond.

'Tammy! Tammy!" he yelled, "Answer me! Please!" he pleads until he noticed the dead stare apparent in her eyes. A scream starts to erupt from the very bottom of his being, as he finds the same lifeless stare in his twenty-five-year-old son's eyes as well. The feeling of anguish in his heart turns into a hatred that is as pure as that of an atheist towards anything claiming divinity. "Show your face!" he screamed, veins bulging in his neck, face blood red, "Show your filthy fucking face!"

"Now see..." Death smiled, walking in front of the Chief, "that's the problem with you muthafuckas... Even in the face of death, you still try to act tough." He sighed as he put his hands in his pockets, "Let's see how far that shit gets you."

"Muthafucka! Do you know who the fuck I am?"

"Besides a dead mean... I could really give two fucks who you were... notice how I used that in the past tense." He laughed.

"Trust me! Once—"

"Your friends find out you're dead?" Death cuts in, arching his eyebrows, "I'll tell you what," he turns the T.V. on. "We're live at the scene of one of the grisliest murders Fort Myers has yet to see since the murder spree of Detective Rodney Mason. As of this moment, I'm standing in front of the house of Narcotics Detective Elvin Willis. Where the police, due to an anonymous tip, found the Detective along with two of his fellow Detectives Thomas Elks and Robert Times... Where they were brutally murdered... Parents, if your children are present, you may want to send them out of the room, due to the graphic details I'm about to report. All three detective's foreheads were riddled with enough bullets to make identifying them impossible, except by their ID's"

"Damn Columbians," Death said, as the reporter continues.

"They were also beheaded."

"That was my idea" explains Death, looking at the Chief with eyes full of fire and a look oh so sinister. Goosebumps appear on the man's arm, despite the unusually warm room.

The Chief looks at Death with in-depth knowledge. The kind of knowledge that only a victim can have when death is certain. The Chief now knows the stores of life flashes before the moment of death are bullshit! The only thing flashing before his eyes is the same scene that was there when he came to... Reality.

"Well... Peep this pimp, I ain't going to go through the whole beheading shit with you. This is how it's going to work. You see this elaborate contraption I've constructed?" said Death, pointing out the fact that the man sits in the middle of a triangle with a point of a very sharp knife pointing at his heart and another behind his neck. With twine tight enough that once released, the knife is sure to almost go through him.

"Now, you've got until someone comes and checks on you" he said, turning to leave. "Oh! By the way!" He spins back around as if he forgot something, "I called the police about two minutes ago... So, they should be pulling up right about now." Death is cut off by the sound of oiled breaks, "Damn, I guess that's the cost of living in such a good neighborhood!" He said, leaving just as suddenly as he came.

After jumping the fence in the backyard and walking calmly to his B.M.W. Death hears the house explode just as his phone rings.

"Hello?"

"Hey, Daddy!"

"Aw! How's Daddy's angel doing?"

"Waiting for you to come home so we can go to Disneyland!"

"Alright, Daddy will be home in about ten minutes, O.K.?"

"O.K. Love you."

"Till death sweetheart."

"Till death, daddy, and beyond."

Neiros Simmons hangs the phone up and takes off his gloves, then slowly puts his seatbelt on, pulling off, just as his iPad chimes notifying him that his off-shores account just received a quarter-million-dollar increase.

"Yeah," he said, into one of the many burner phones he owns, specifically for business.

"What gon my yut!"

"Wha gon?"

"Just a lil business,"

"What kind?"

"Well... I got a job for you."

"O.K."

"I need you to clean the house of Oscar Venosula."

5

"The pay?"

"Your rate!"

"Good answer, for a house so big... Ten dollars an hour" Death said, informing the man the hit will cost him one hundred thousand dollars.

"Done."
"Confirmation number?"

"Just give me a heads up." He replies, letting him know how to send him the mark's head.
For ten an hour, I'll give you a day's notice of completion" remarks Death, informing the Jamaican he'll send the whole body.

"Now my yut!" The man laughs, "A heads up will do!"

"Done."

Now... You've got an introduction to some of my world. But, listen to this crazy shit. Oscar, the muthafucka I'm about to behead! Yeah, he's the Columbian that sent me to merc the Police Chief and friends, but shit! Ain't nobody above death, and for the right amount, even the buyer can get it.... but I'm about to take y'all on a serious ride. All you need to do is hold on.

Chapter 2

Two weeks later...

N ow, this is that bullshit!" I said as I stared at the financial projections for the previous month. Yeah, I'm a businessman in many aspects. At this moment, I'm Nerios Simmons, president, and C.E.O. of False Reality Records. Sitting in the plus office of my label's building, going over the record sales of all my artists. I realize... Shit!
Something isn't clicking! Sales are down like a muthafucka!

"Tivia! What's this bullshit?" I exclaim to my vice president, Tivia Alcontaro. This sexy ass Puerto Rican chick with a figure you'd swear she paid for! Sometimes I look at her small waist, 48" ass, and think maybe she did buy that shit, but she didn't. At least that's what she says.

"Jizzle, to be honest, I have the slightest idea of what's up. Maybe we need to recruit some new talent." She said, calling me by my nickname, as I said, I've got a lot of them.

"Yeah" I steeple my fingers, "maybe we do... Maybe we do."

"Mr. Simmons." The intercom in my office comes to life as the lovely voice of my secretary flows out of the speaker,

"What's up Tiffany?"

"A Mr. Johnson is here for a 1:30 appointment."

"Send him in" I reply as a tall white male walks through the door, dressed in urban gear from head to toe.

To be honest, in my opinion, some white boys just can't do the whole urban thing, but this one is pulling it off. "Ummm... What can I do for you, Mr. Johnson?"

"Murder."

"Murder?"

"Yeah, that's my name... Murder," he states, as a matter of fact, staring at me intently with intense green eyes.

"And you do what?"

"Murder shit."

"Murder shit! Hmmm... Well, I don't see any guns or knives on you. So, I'm going to assume you mean on beats and shit."

"Yeah... Whateva."

"Well, Murder, is it? Ima keep it one hundred with you. The one white-boy I've heard that I'll sign is already making millions."

"Well... I ain't no Eminem"

"No shit! Most muthafuckas ain't."

"Listen... I ain't on no bashing faggots and dissing my mom type of shit! I'm a dope boy and a jack boy! That's what I do and that's what my music is about!"

Is this cracka serious! I mean just sitting here looking at his ass and me murdering him on the premise of how he looks

8

comes to mind, "Well," I pause, with a sigh, "You got some shit for me to hear?"

"Hell yeah!" He said, pulling out a C.D., that Tivia takes, placing it into my sound system. At first, an alright beat comes on, then:
you know I murder shit, gotta murder shit/ Comes to the blow, Murder gone move the shit/ 36 white bitches, 16 Mexicans/ standing on ya block moving snow call me avalanche/ Weed come in caravans, keep a 40 by my side/ Come sideway at me, 40 make ya brains slide—

Damn! This cracka might be marketable!

"Question? How long you've been rapping?"

"Shit homey... I'm a be honest wit ya, the only reason I'm in your office is cause my niggas say my shit tight, ya feel me... Me personally, I'm a street nigga, been in dem streets since I was a jit, ya feel me. I could care less if you like my shit or not. This ain't my life. So if not, fuck it."
Now normally, under any other circumstances, I would've slapped the shit out of this crack, just to see where his heart is. As a matter of fact, going with my first mind. I stand up calmly walking up to him. Once I'm in a rage, I do just as I said. I should've fired this muthafucka up! I've got to give the muthafucka props. As soon as my hand connects with his face. He immediately shoots an ugly jab at me, but I easily weave that shit, stepping to the side out of range, to the sound of Tivia cocking her pistol, placing it inches from Murder's face.

"What the fuck?" he sounds, breathing hard with anger.

9

"This is the fuck!" I state, with force, yet in a calm voice. "Even though my label is called False Reality, we ain't living in none! If you just some white boy that heard a couple of Jeezy, Frank Lini, and Plies songs, and think you living a gangsta life, this ain't the spot for ya."

"I ain't gone stand here and cut up, if you think that's what's going to happen. Tell shawty to drop the pistol and we can bump." Murder said, with what I guess was supposed to be his serious face.

"Now that is funny! Listen and listen good. Not saying I wouldn't bump with you, but last time I check, I was worth enough money to buy you and twenty muthafuckas that think like you! If I wanted to, I could make it to where the only one that'll know your whereabouts is God... So why would I waste a second of my expensive breath on you?"

I guess the realization of my words set in, because Murder's murderous look evaporated, and he turned around, heading for the door.

"Hey Murder" I call out to him. "Be in the studio tomorrow at
8 am... Tiffany will give you directions."

"Bet that." He states, on his way out.
You see, the reason I decided to give him a chance was that it takes a real man to just take what I dished out to him. Most muthafuckas would've tried to prove how hard they are. Without keeping in mind one principle.

A man that continues to fight in the face of defeat, is not brave, but a fucking idiot. Not everybody that retreats is a coward, and most people that continue to fight in the face of adversity, are defeated not because they were overpowered, but because they felt they had something to prove.

In some cases, it was that they had enough courage to endure. In others, it was that they were more intelligent than their adversary, but who possesses more wisdom. The man that runs, regroups, and lives another day, in the end defeating his enemies, or the man that in the name of courage, morals, and bravery dies with the title: Here lies that brave, courageous, morally intact man, engraved on his tombstone, food for thought.

***

Later on that day, I had to slide by one of my traps. Yeah, Jizzle sells dope too. Why do you think my label is called False Reality? I got about three different realities going on! All of them real to me, but to anybody else, you'd catch hell trying to convince them otherwise.

Now, all my niggas in my traps know I run the record label, but the whole hitman shit, that's my lil secret. Now, my wife Sienna and my lil girl, have the slightest idea about the dope or the murder. So, you see why I named my label False Reality, reality is whatever I deem it to be.
I'm not going to lie, it's a pleasant day as I pull up to the trap. A couple of clouds in the sky. I think it's about 85 degrees, but looking around the hood, the only thing pleasant is the sky and most muthafuckas ain't looking up so they could give two fucks about the limit the sky shows them. Which is there ain't none. I guess that's why I am the way I am, and they are who they are. Me, I look at the sky and realize one thing, if the clouds appear to be close, yet are in

11

reality so far away. That means that I only perceive myself as a fuck up and confine myself to the lowest. Then I can't be mad when I die in the hood as a street hustler. In other words, you don't have to sell dope to sell dope. Outsource, it's the American Way.

"Jizzle! Brah, what brings you this way?" says Gut One, my captain over all of my traps. I know you're probably thinking how this nigga gets a name like Gut One.

Now based on the previous situations, you'll more than likely think it's some killer-type shit. Naw, this nigga will put his dick in anything tricking. To be honest, she doesn't have to be tricking, but willing, but that's my nigga. Plus, he might as well buy stocks in Lifestyles as many condoms as he buys.

"You know a nigga gotta slide through and check the trap, my nigga!" I say walking up and embracing him.

After we greet each other and walk towards the house, I pause for a second as the door opens and this fine ass sister stands in the doorway, in some short cutting ass shorter and a halter top. The thighs on shawty so thick, you'd swear when she talks walking them short ass shorts going to catch fire. Not to mention, ma got some illegal shit between her legs.
Looking like she's snuggling Pitbull puppies in dem shorts.

I can tell this ain't your regular hood bitch. Don't get me wrong, she dressed for the streets, but there is something in them honey brown eyes, and just the ora ma is shooting off her that says...oh shit, this bitch police!

"Yo Jizzle," Gut One says, "This is —"

"Akema. Akema Tiara." Shawty said, with nothing but pure seduction in her eyes, as she walks out of the house and down the stairs. Each motion confirms my thoughts.

You see, a real street nigga knows when a bitch isn't from the streets. Take this bitch! She would've been straight if not for the outfit. She tried to go for the hood bitch, dope boy groupie role. Which most chicks are. You know em, always buying the shortest shit they can find the mall has to offer, in the hopes some nigga with a little bit of cash will scoop em up.

She had the look down to a science, but it's the walk. You see, shawties in the hood walk like fucking is a job, not just a pastime. Like as soon as they came out of the womb. Their momma gave them a Beyonce video. Know what I'm talking about?

Not this bitch, she glides down the stairs trying to put too much into her walk. Shawties round my way don't have to try. As soon as they get up off the sofa and slide across the living room, a nigga dick in em before they can open the refrigerator and get some juice.

"Akema Tierra, huh?" I said, thinking about how I gotta play this situation. "Where did you find a name like that?"

"My momma."
"Oh, this bitch got jokes. What's your nationality?"

"Nigga."

13

"Hmm...with a name like that," I said, trying to keep my cool because truly, this bitch is starting to get on my damn nerves. Being I think this bitch is the feds though. I ain't gone push her pretty ass nose out the back of her head.

"So Neiros" She smiles, "I guess you're not going to introduce yourself?"

"Shit, you already know my name. So, why go through the bullshit" I shrug, "Yo, Gut One, I'm about to slide."

"Already? You just got here homey."

"Yeah, check with me later... I gotta go feed Eddie and Demos."

"You still fighting dem two." He replies, picking up the code I just spit on him about Akema. That's why he's my captain. "Yeah, bout fifteen a fight."

"Well, I'm a check and see if I can find some fights for em."

"Ten four... That's what I do homey."

"Oh... So you fight dogs?" Akema asks.

"Mhm"

"Is it to the death?" She said, putting a little bit too much emphasis on the last word.

"Sometimes. Other times just till it's over"
"Yeah, well only like watching a death math."

14

"Mhm," I reply, cocking my head to the side, thinking, maybe this bitch ain't the feds, and got some other angle. If so, I may need to stick around for a minute.

"Gut One... You burning?"

"What about your dogs?" questions Akema.

"They'll be okay. Brah you burning?"

"Does a rabbit turn brown when a bear uses it for toilet paper?"

"What? Where do you get that square ass shit from? Man, let's slide! Does a rabbit…this nigga tripping!"

As we walk inside, Akema manages to make sure she stays in front of me so I can see that ass bounce. Damn this bitch fine!

"Hello?" Gut One says into his cellphone.
"Alright. That's what it do. Mm hmm. Uh huh…okay…
One. Yo Jizzle, that was my baby momma, you feel me. Tomeka is sick and I gotta bring her some medicine, you can watch the trap for about an hour?"

'Damn homey!" I said, not really wanting to be alone with this bitch "Yeah, Yeah, I got ya!"

"Bet that. I'll be back A.S.A.P." He said, fleeing the house.

Once Gut One is gone, I go and find some trees and blunts, rolling up. The entire time Akema is watching me like I got a steak on my ass or something. I wanna snap, but real G's

15

keep it cool in the summer, and I'm cold enough to walk in snow barefoot without getting frost bite.

"So," I start, "What's your angle shawty?"

"I ain't got no angle. I'm all vertical baby."

"Baby? Since when did I start shrinking to the point you could call me a baby?"

"So defensive!"

"If that's the title you wanna put on it... I call it being serious, but back to square one. You ain't no street bitch, so what are you doing on the northside of Duval County, in my trap dressed like you trying to fuck something?"

"Maybe I am, trying to fuck something." She said, looking at me like a lioness looks at their prey.

"Mm hmm, Let's see then!" with that said, I pull out my .45 and look Akema in the eyes, "Bust it open."
To my astonishment, the bitch swiftly pulls them short ass shorts off, and before me sits one of the prettiest juice boxes I've ever seen.

After a slight pause, I slowly walk over to Akema, checking to make sure nothing is in the chamber, and slowly slide the barrel of my .45 in that shit.

"Ooohhh, Cold Steel!" She pants.

I increase the speed of my thrust, growing hard as fuck as Akema starts throwing that pussy back against my steel. I look in astonishment at her juices glistening on my pistol. I'm so locked in on her fucking my pistol. I'm blown when I look up and find she's stripped all of her clothes off, exposing her size C breast, as she massages her hard nipples.

"Oh shit! Oh shit! Keep fucking me, baby! Harder! Faster! Har— Oh! My! God!"

Oh shit! This bitch just bust a nut on my pistol! I'm talking about Niagra Falls! She got Jizzle fucked up!

I hurry up and strip down to my socks, commencing to pounding the fuck outta Akema's ass. In one minute, I got this bitch trying to run from a nigga, but I lock on that ass like a pit and bust all in that bitch!

"Damn! God! Damn!" She pants, 'Boy! God! Damn!"

"God ain't got shit to do with it shawty... Now, get ya ass dressed. We gotta talk." I said, grabbing my pants and keeping it one hundred. I'm really hoping Ma got the right answers... Cause even good ass pussy ain't above death.

***

The melodic voice of Sade glides out of Tivia's sound system as she sings about a smooth operator. Tivia sits in front of her coffee table with almost a quarter ounce of cocaine on the glass. Throwing her head back and sniffled hard.

She knows if Jizzle ever found out about her cocaine habit, most likely he'd fire her ass, if not kill her on sight. To be honest, it's only out of respect for him that she hides her addiction.

"Hello?" she said, answering her phone.

"Ah... Tivia! My niece! How are you?"

"Uncle Tito!! Long time no hear, you must bring some good news." Tivia said, knowing that more than likely it's the opposite.

"Actually, I wish the news was good," Tito said confirming her thoughts.

"What has Temero done now?" Tivia asks, referring to her brother.

"No, no. Temero is fine, it's your Papa."

"What about Papa? Is he okay?"

"Tivia, my sweetheart, your Papa is dead."

"Dead?? How?"

"We think it's a hit from the Jamaicans. We're not one hundred percent sure, but we'll know soon."

"Well, what do you need from me?"Tivia chokes out, tears in her voice.
"We need you on the next flight back to Columbia."

"Back to Columbia?" She jocks upright, "But, but, why?"

"Your brother is the next in command, so..." Tito lets the last word dangle for emphasis.

"Aw shit" Tivia puts her face in her palm, knowing full well what her uncle is implying. 'Why can't you step in uncle, you as well as I know what Temero is about to do."

"Yes, this is true. But it is his birthright and I am in no position to strip him of his right to rule. This is why I ask that you come home."

"Yeah, yeah! To possibly talk some sense into him. But uncle I have a life here, I have loyalties."

"Tivia! What are these loyalties? Tell me what it is this life you talk about! You are the daughter of Oscar Venosula! Your loyalty is to your family! Your life is one short of royalty!"

"But, but uncle, this is not something I asked for. I am happy with my life as it is. Yet, you are right. My loyalties with my blood are stronger than that of my life here, yet... I am not leaving to come back, only to attempt to talk some sense into—" Boom!

The sound of a large caliber gun cuts Tivia's words short.

"Uncle! Tito!" She screams into the phone.

"Hel-lo Tivia my dear sister."

"Temero! What have you done?"

"You should know the old American saying "Out with the old...in with the new. I think it is."
"Uncle Tito?" Tivia asks, her hand shaking with rage.

"Why Temero? WHY!"

"The old ones were too passive in my opinion, it's time this family rules with an iron fist!"

"Hmm. You know what they say about opinions my dear brother."

"Yeah, Yeah. The whole asshole metaphor, but listen here sister. The only opinions that matter in this world are those of the strong."

"And why is that?"

"Because the strong take what they want. While the weak sit and wait for the scraps. Enough of this back-and-forth banter.
Whose side are you on?"

"First, one question."

"That is?"

"Who killed father?" Tivia turns to walk towards her bedroom, the door explodes open and two armed assailants enter, spraying the now empty living room.

Tivia immediately grabs her pistol off the nightstand and gets into a low crouch. It's moments like these her father prepared her for in the mountains of Columbia. As the men slowly creep into her room, Tivia forces all other thoughts out of her head, placing all her attention on the door.
Coming up with a better plan, she uses the mirror above her bed to reflect the red beam on the bottom of her as Heckler and Koch head towards the door.

The men enter the room. The beam on the mirror causes them to think Tivia is directly in front of them. They quickly let about ten shells fly free of the clips holding them.

Seeing her plan in effect, Tivia places two well-placed shots to the heads of the men, ending their time in this world. Standing calmly, she reaches for her phone, knowing her brother is still on the line.

"Temero."

"Still here, sis."

"I'll be home soon."

"Well, I'll be waiting."

"So what do we have to talk about?" Akema asks, sitting on her legs on the sofa. I am not going to lie. I really, really hope shawty is legit because I'm gonna hate having to kill such a beautiful woman.

"Listen," I said, allowing the smoke from my mouth to cause that pause in a sentence that sometimes is so important to get a point across. "I'ma be very blunt wit ya Akema, you ain't no hood bitch. So to me, you might be the feds or something." I pull on my blunt, "Now, here's the catch. If I feel you're lying to me; I am going to kill you...if I feel you're telling me the truth, I'm just gonna fuck you again and we can talk about putting you on the team."
Akema puts her feet on the floor, leaning back, letting out of the most seductive laughs I've heard in a long time. Really, this woman got some real swag about herself. The way she tosses her head back. All the way to the way her long silky

21

hair flips to the side when she brings her head forward and sets them beautiful eyes on me. With a look that says, she'd eat me alive. She tells me she's seen some of the finer things this life has to offer, and this hood façade is just a means to some end.

"Jizzle!" She continues to laugh, 'Boy, you are a riot! Me... The feds! Really? Me!" She points to herself, "Boy, I can understand you're being somewhat cautious of me, but trust me. I am no threat to you or your lifestyle Death."

"Death? And who would that be?" I said, trying to keep my cool. I really want to just flip the bitch, and be done with it, but that would be an amateur mistake.

It is an insane move for one to end any source of information without draining it. That's the equivalent of buying a book and burning it before reading it.

"Come on Neiros." Her tone changes, making me uneasy.

"You mustn't play the ignorant role; we are above that, way above that. But, just to break the ice some, my name is Akema Tiara, daughter of Syrena Tiara, wife of Tim Hunter, brother of —"

'Terrance Hunter?" I cut in, my heart pounding, "Teacher of Neiros Simmons...hmm. I thought Hunter was dead."

"And he is... I've been trying to find you for years now, the last time we saw each other I was ten and you thirteen..."

"Mm... hmm, so what brings you here now?"

"You, I've traveled the world since that young age, but this pussy has been throbbing for you... No matter who I've been with, even though I've never been with you. The reality was, they weren't you."

"Mmhmm, so what brings you here now?" I point at the ground for emphasis.

"Position."

"Position?"

"Yes, position."

"Which one?"

"Whatever position you choose for me to play... I know you've got wifey at home and I'm cool with that... I can play my position."

"Yeah, that shit sounds good, damn good. But this is real life, you actually think I'm going to sit here and you- a woman that has just confessed to a lifelong obsession with me- is going to just sit on the side and not allow feelings to get involved?

"What are feelings?" Akema asks.

"Feelings are a state of mind. Only able to control the weak of heart and the slow of mind. They are the preverbal water faucet that only the master plumber can turn on and turn off."

"With Hunter as my teacher, would it be possible for me to become a master plumber?"

"No." I state matter of fact, "...because if you took heed to Hunter's teachings, an obsession with me would've been impossible." I said thinking about one of my mentor's last lessons.

"Listen Neiros," Hunter said, till this day it still amazes me how this midnight black man could contain so much insight into life. It's hard to explain, even for me, but if someone saw this 6'1" black man, with his dreadlocks hanging, it would be hard to believe he could as fast as he does, or that the words coming out of his mouth are his.

"Most human beings walking the Earth are so misguided, it's a shame. The reason being, their sense of worth, their concept of emotion, their total outlook on life... For emotions are just what the word says... e-motion. Energy in motion. Now, who is in control of this energy? For some, it's all of the things outside of themselves. For me, it's me. If you were to ask any modern-day psychologist about a person that can kill without emotion, they would say that there is something wrong with him mentally. True... and not true... For me, once I have come to the point of murder, my energy is in full control. The reason I don't feel any sympathy or sadness, or shit, madness for that matter. It is because I control that energy and do not allow it to affect the task at hand. Do you know what happens to emotional people? They die a horrible death. Why? Because they fear death. That is your mission Neiros, to control and become what people fear most. Death is inevitable, but it does not affect those who don't fear it. Why? Or had someone scared you? What do you feel? You feel your heart rate increase and that sinking feeling only fear can give you. Once you learn to control fear, the rest will fall in place. Same with love. One should never love someone or something they fear they could lose. Why? Your enemies, those true enemies...will use what you fear most against you. Therefore, if you have no fear of losing anything you love and truly believe the creator chose that moment in time to take it, what can the world use against you?

"Are you sure that's true?" Akema said, bringing me back to the present moment.

"The question is, can you prove otherwise?" I reply, in an attempt to wipe the smile off that beautiful face, but contrary to my attempt, Akema continues to smile, glancing over to Gut One's T.V. setup. I would've said walk, but that one word can't put enough visual concept on the way the beautiful creation strides in front of me.

After putting in a D.V.D., she obviously had concealed it in her purse. To my amazement, the face of the one man who I can say has the right to say he raised me, appears on the T.V. screen.

"Neiros," Hunter said, with a look on his face that almost made me absolutely believe he know I am listening to his voice and seeing his face. "My son, pupil, and only confidant. If you are seeing this, that means Akema has accomplished what she was told to do. She has also informed you of the fact that you've been an obsession of hers since her youth, but..." And the pause is so dramatic and long, I already know where the next few statements are heading...I was slipping,

"If you actually allowed the word obsession to define her state of mind, in the words of Jesus, as long as I have been with you and yet you still do not know. Neiros I'm pretty

25

sure you've seen the movie Coming to America. In this movie, a woman was groomed for the prince, to think, act accordingly, before you say it, you're welcome."

With those words, the screen goes dark. That's the thing about Hunter, he'll never give you 100%. The rest is for you to figure out.

"So," I said, looking at Akema, "You'll play your position to the tee?"

"From Hunter would you expect less?"

"Of course not," I said as Gut One came rushing in the house followed by two masked men.

Now, I know this is going to sound like some arrogant shit, but do you know the first thought that came to my mind... I know damn well these niggas ain't about to rob Death! I mean really! But low and behold within the next minute. Here I am with a pistol to my head.

"Get flat fuck nigga!" one of the masked men said, attempting to push me on the floor.

As I was about to comply with his order, one of the most unusual things I have ever encountered took place,

"Oooohhh!" went Akema.

"Bitch! What the fuck you got going on?" states the other masked man.

"Fucking... Fucking is the only thing on my mind... I knew these niggas was soft and y'all just proved me right!" said

Akema, standing rubbing her hands between her legs, playing into the eyes of these amateurs. The reason I label them is that, any real killer would've merced her ass for moving.

"Just chill shawty." The man said, lust in his eyes, "After I handle these two fuck niggas, I got ya, just chill!" He said, allowing her to get a little too up close and personal in my opinion.

And just like I figured, his second head became his weakness. With eyes on me, all of a sudden, they enlarge two times their size, and he turns, looking into Akema's face. Which has one of those devious smiles on it, for a woman of such beauty, it's quite chilling.

The man looks down, going into panic mode, as the sight of Akema's knife sticking out of his chest reveals the fact she's gut him from the navel up.

He had just enough time to complete a few thoughts. Damn, that is either one sharp-ass knife or Akema is strong as fuck! And where the fuck did she get the knife from?

That distraction was all I needed to take out the other assailant with a swift sweep, and in the same motion, regaining my footing so I could disarm him, shooting him at point-blank range in the face. Which is a big mistake, because now I have blood, skull, and brain matter on an outfit that could probably pay somebody's rent for three months!

"Aww! Boo, you ruined your brand-new outfit!" Akema said, in a mocking tone.

"Actually, it ain't brand new... Just looks that way, but Gut One! What the fuck?"

"What? Jizzle, this shit is all yo fault!" Gut One said, and with the look he's giving Akema, I can honestly agree with him, I was slipping. This bitch had my full attention. I would blame that shit on Hunger, but in my heart, I know that's just a cop-out move.

So I take that "Yeah Gut, I was slipping."

"Yeah! All these cameras and you let these niggas get the jump on me! Damn! What! This bitch pussy, gold?"

"Alright... Brah, I get it! I fucked up!" I said, really getting tired of Gut One's attitude, but knowing it ain't over by a longshot.

"Now nigga! Fuck that! If I had my nose wide open bout some bitch, you'd be on my ass just as bad!"

"Jizzle," I said, glad my cellphone saved me.

"What it is bitch?" my homeboy Javier said, on the other line.

Now, this young nigga is wild as fuck. We met in prison about five years back. I told him I would keep in contact with his ass, but you know how that shit is. Now don't get it twisted, Jizzle keeps it one hundred. I was fucking with him for a while, but with me trying to get right. Time didn't permit constant contact, but with real niggas, not muthafuckas who claim they real, real niggas, ain't got to be in contact every day. They still fuck with each other from a distance. I and Javier caught back up when he started fucking with this chick from the Ville named My'Asia. I heard about the shawty in the assassin circle, but I'll off that shawty if she even swang my way.

"Some old shit," I replied.

"Shit! I'm just swinging through and thought maybe I'd slide your way..."

"Naw, naw, you might wanna holla at a nigga."

"Some serious shit."
"Yep."

"Bout?"

"My-Asia."

"And?"

"I'd rather tell you in person brah."

"Listen, if that bitch..."

"Now, it ain't got nothing to do with her directly... Man! Just come meet me at ya crib in about thirty!"

"Make that an hour."

"Right."
After hanging up with Javier, I look over to find Gut One with Akema bend over, pounding this bitch from the back,

"Gut! What the fuck brah?"

"Brah!" he said, breathing hard, "You ain't never slipping! If this bitch pussy that good, I had to get some!"
"You couldn't wait until after we clean this shit up?" I said with a grin on my face.

"Shiiittt! Dem fuck niggas dead, they'll be alright. Plus, I called Sam and Tony while you was on the phone, so you can slide." He said, placing his attention back on Akema.

Sam and Tony do clean-up. The best I've yet to see. I don't know what they do with the bodies, but I know I ain't got to worry about nobody but God knowing where they at, except for Sam and Tony.

As I'm about to slide, I hear Akema tell Gut One to hold up, "Jizzle! We got unfinished business."

"True... I got some business to handle, but if what you told me is true, I shouldn't have to find you."

"Oh trust me! You won't." Akema said, with very serious eyes and right then something told me, Hunter sent me my Eve.

Chapter 3

Life stands up stretching as the sun declines behind the horizon traveling to another part of the world. Walking into the bathroom, turning the shower on almost scolding. Life undresses, stepping in the water as if it's only lukewarm. Most people in Life's profession ask how the name came about. The answer is so simple, most of the time they laugh if a lie is being told.

Life is an assassin. One of the best in the business. The reason the name Life was given, is each one of Life's victims beg for their Life to be taken; and sometimes the wish is granted, yet in granting the wish, the victim ends up as a vegetable for life.

So even as an assassin, Life is a giver of life, not a taker... Sometimes.

The sound of the telephone causes Life to walk at a mid-stride out of the bathroom, "Hello?"

"Ah! Life."

"Edward."

"Still playing the family role?"

"As always."

"Up for a little fun?"

"As always."

"Oh, trust me. This is going to be the assignment of your life."

"Who's the mark?"

"Death."

"As in... THE Death?"

"The one and only."

"Location?"

"Don't have it."

"Picture?"

"Nonexistent."

"How am I supposed to find him then."

"That's the tricky part... But the payoff is five million dollars." "Five million dollars?"

"Yep... spread amongst six investors."

"Really?"

"Really."

"Your commission?"

"Paid."

"So... Wil you take the job?"

"Consider Death... Dead."
Forty-five minutes later, after I went to one of the many houses I've chased in the city, showered, and changed clothes. I decided to switch from the Benz to the Yamaha and head to my apartment in the Arlington area of the city named Aston Ridge.

One thing life has taught me, nothing happens by chance, and nobody can receive 100% of your trust in a short amount of time. Yet even the word "trust" by my standards, may be twisted in the sign of others.

The way I see it, if you trust someone, to only be capable of certain things. You lessen the chances of them breaking your trust.

For instance, man by nature is infallible, by nature. So they are prone to make mistakes. So me, I trust my niggas enough that
I know there is a possibility they'll fuck up somewhere along the line.

The problem most people have is they put too much trust in the one around them to the point where one simple mistake is a breach of trust. In essence, that's a fucked-up burden to put on one man's shoulders. Because now he's forced to walk around and critique every aspect of his relation with his so called friend or loved one.

So me, I trust enough to give full trust, if that makes any sense to you. That's why I can fuck with Javier. Like right now, as I pull up to my apartment, he's doing what I trust

him to do. Talk to women. Would I be doing the same thing? No, because I hate unwanted attention, nor is it needed, but in
Javier's case. I know he's on point, and once I get off the Yamaha. It's proven.

"So," Javier said, to some thick white chick, "I guess yo busta ass homeboys over there think shit sweet or something... So they sent you over here to get some info, or to distract."
"What are you talking about?" She responds, one of them busted in the act looks on her face.

"Ya two homeboys under the stairs over there," replies Javier, going under his shirt, pulling out his Taurus nine miller equipped with a red beam. Grabbing the button on the pistol grip, he points the beam directly on the chest of one of the would-be jack boys.

"Whoa! Whoa! Homie! You got dot!" The man with the red beam on his shirt exclaims.

"Ight" Javier smirks, "Just telling y'all know shit real over here... You know. Stopping a lot of unnecessary bloodsheds." He said, putting the pistol back under his shirt. Then turning to the girl, "But back to you."

"I'm sorry Money, but —"

"Hold up... Ain't no need to apologize, if I was offended, I'd whacked your dog ass right here... You were just a pawn in a dirty chest game."

"So, you think you can trust me?" She smiles.

"Uh uh, I know I can't."

"But you still gone fuck wit me?"

"Of course. Cause I can do one thing you or your busta ass homeboys can't."

"What's that?"

"Blow ya brains out and go up the street to that lil Italian restaurants and eat some spaghetti and meatballs, extra sauce." He said, still smiling, "So... What's happenings? You busy tonight?"

"Um, yeah. I'm busy." The girl replies. The realization of exactly what she is dealing with registering on her face.

"Ight, then get yo dog ass on. Jizzle! What's happening nigga?"

"The question should be what are you up to?" I gesture to the girl.

"You know how it is homie... Sometimes bitches think shit sweet. To be honest, I spared their ass. I got the silencer kit in the glove compartment."

"Brah... You bugged the fuck out! Let's slide before you fuck around and hurt somebody."

"Yeah, I'm a bug alright... Mr. let's hurt everybody."

"Why you gotta bring up old shit?"

"Brah... I did a year on C.M. bout that old shit!"

"I ain't said that. Loyalty told me I gotta ride... But "He holds his finger up," That still doesn't change the fact you are a bug too." He said, taking me back three years.

"Javier!" I said, sliding in his cell, "Aye, I got some shit I gotta go handle. So I'm a need you to hold this sack down... If these crackas catch a nigga I'm going to C.M."
"Brah... What the fuck you talking about?" He said, rubbing the sleep out of his eyes.

"This fuck nigga Nut owe a nigga two hundred... I guess he think shit sweet or something."

"Ight, go handle that nigga. Slide, I got you." He started putting his shoes on.

"See, it ain't that simple. If I just merc that nigga, I might have to worry about his niggas, right? So, all dem niggas in the same room... You know, slide. Hit dem niggas up, slide out."

"How many?" He sighs.

"Three."

"What?"

"Brah... I've been studying des niggas. Once I hit Nut, dem niggas going into panic mode. While they panicking, I'm stabbing!"

"You wit the bullshit." He said.

"What's up?"

"Let's ride."

"Ight."

"Damn! You sure nigga?"

"Hell no, you said it! Let's slide!"
"Nigga I'm bullshitting, let's slide!"
Once me and Javier tie our knives to our hands, we calmly walk downstairs with our coffee mugs. Talking like nothing's wrong.

The crazy thing is the act is all for nothing. One thing about prison, niggas feel the tension in the air like it's an electric force. So as we walk, niggas are already watching to see the action. As soon as we get to Nut's room, we rush off into the cell.

I hit Nut two times and start on the other nigga, as Javier hits the last one up. Once we finish, we walk out and head back upstairs. But snitches come to prison too, and the next day we was on our way to confinement. Not to mention, one of the soft ass niggas we hit up. Wrote a statement on us. Pussy ass nigga!

"So," I said to Javier, "What's this important business you've been wanting to tell me about?"

"Oh, that shit... Well, you know My'Asia on that hitman shit... So, how about she called me and said yo name came across the wire."

"Hmmm," I replied. This is actually really interesting. Nobody besides my handler, Hunter, his brother, and now Akema know I was Death. So somebody wants Nerios dead... Amazing, but it's possible.

"Yeah," Javier said.

"Did she take the contract?"

"On the strength of me... Naw."
"Does she have a name?"

"Yep, some chico named Diego."

"Aw shit! So, this is how he wants to play it."

"You know buddy?"

"Know of. Here's the situation, in total, I've got bout ten traps spread around Duval. The only two muthafuckas in the dope game going harder than me is Smoke and Iblis... Diego, can't take out Smoke. That D9 shit strapped like the military. But, if he can get me out of the way, he can make enough cash to go
at Iblis."

"Bruh... Question, why are you on this dope shit anyway? You doing good with the music shit."

"True." I said, "I got a lot of reasons... The main one, all my niggas can't rap and are going to be hustling for life. In a lot of ways, the only way I can help dem niggas is with dope."

The thing is, that's a sad reality as it pertains to urban society. Most of the males don't have any skills to make it in the legit world, therefore they turn to a life of crime, then you have the ones that are not in it for the money, but for the fame.

"Yeah," Javier responds. "Well, I got to handle some business, so yo shit got a back door?"

"Yeah... why?"

"Trust me." He said, looking out the blinds. "Niggas think this shit is sweet."

"Ight." I shrug my shoulders.

After Javier left, I sat down and thought about how to handle Diego. One thing I don't do well is let lifestyles class. So, to go at him as Death, could in the long run be a major mistake. I got to handle this dude because if nobody else doesn't, I love Jizzle.

After locking the door, deciding to head home, I walk outside to a murder scene. At first, I see the white girl's brains all over the sidewalk. Then, I look at the entire scene. I see the two dudes with her dead in the same hallway they were in. Right before they zip the body bag up, I see the mask on their faces.

"Yo!" Javier said, answering his cellphone.

"You straight?"

"Oh yeah... I'm good. At the Italian restaurant up the street, eating me some spaghetti and meatballs, extra sauce."

***

After talking to Javier, I got on my Yamaha, heading home. You know one of the main defenses I have, my enigmatic character. To be honest, there ain't much I've revealed to anyone.

Well, now's a better time than any. I was born on December 10th, 1982, to the proud parents of Regina Simmons and Charles Simmons.

The thing is, both of my parents were in the streets. My mom was a prostitute, while my pops sold dope. Once I got older, I asked my pops one day. Why he allowed my mom to sell her pussy and his answer changed my life forever.

He told me my mom was doing the same thing now, the day he met her. He tried his hardest to get her out of the streets, but little did he know, all the men before her convinced her to do the same, only to abandon her later. Some a year, others more than that, but he told himself he would prove he was not all the other men in her life. It took him fifteen years, but one day she came home and told him she was done with the streets.

His answer showed me two things. One: Something special is always worth waiting for and fighting for. Even though my mom sold pussy, she stood by my pop's side through two prison bids and a whole lot of bullshit. Two: A man's word is his bond to whatever life he receives. All of my mom's previous men left her only to never find someone like her again. So being that their word wasn't shit, as so is their life.

By the time I was thirteen, I was doing my thing! One other lesson my parents taught me, a man who chooses to never learn anything, shouldn't be mad when he has nothing. So, in school, I was a sponge. I soaked up everything. The same with the streets. So, by thirteen, I was selling dope and doing little legal side jobs.

After high school, I went to prison, got a degree, opened my label, and continued trapping. As for the whole hitman situation, I met Hunter at the age of 11. I've seen martial arts movies, but he was the first black man I'd ever seen in the hood doing some Bruce lee type shit. Me, being curious, wonders in his yard one day, and the rest is history.

He was a hitman at the time and on my seventeenth birthday. He puts me on to my first hit. Some dope boy on the southside into these cats for about fifty racks. After being trained by Hunter, I took to murder like a fish to water, and the ten grand I made, made it that much easier. From that point, the rest is history.

Pulling up to my home in San Marco, I can only think about how far I've come. Shit, most people from my area got life or died on the same streets they claim they love. I guess that is what sets me apart from them. I don't love the streets. How can a sane man love destruction? Now, I love certain aspects of being in the streets. Like the awareness I've gained from being in certain situations, but can I say I love selling dope? That would be stupid! I love the money I receive from selling dope.

All that and more goes away the moment I open the door and see my daughter, Natasha's face. Now, this is what matters... Natasha. My wife, Sienna. I would be lying if I said I didn't love her, but in love with her... now.

But, as this Spanish and African American beauty strides my way in a pair of hip-hugging jeans, that look like they're painted on her lower body, forcing her thighs to show with each step, the well-toned muscles she's received from hours in the gym. I can't help but look into them hazel, eyes, scanning down to her perfect size b breast, knowing with certainty, that as much as I love her, I lust for her more than anything else. Me and Si met when I was eighteen and had an aspiration of attending college. She was standing outside of her car looking beautiful as she pouted about being locked out.

"Need some help?" I asked, walking up.

"Umm, no I'm good!" She replied, giving me one of the meanest expressions I'd seen until that point in my life.

"Well, it sure it looks like you could use some help."

"Okay... Listen here Thugs-R-Us," She rolled her eyes, which I honestly found cute. "I am not some little damsel in distress that needs a knight in shining armor. As a matter of fact, my boyfriend is on his way as we speak."
"Oh, you think I'm a thug?" I said amused, for she had my attention at the words I am not instead of I ain't, which showed me she's educated.

"Really!" She snapped.

Really what?" I smiled, with my hands in my pockets.

"Am I going to have to pull my mace out or scream in order to get rid of you? Oh, let me guess, you weren't taught the meaning of the word no before you dropped out huh?"

"Well," She said, in a schoolteacher's voice. "N and O spells no, which means you cannot have whatever it is you want... Therefore, you can go home now. Okay, little boy." In most cases, I would've snapped on her ass, but the arrogant side of me told me I could get this bitch.

So a month later, I'm at this party on the southside, and she just so happens to be there with her boyfriend. "Hey! School teacher!" I said, walking up on her and her boyfriend.

"Oh my god! Not you again!" She exclaimed, rolling her eyes.

"What Sienna... You know Neiros?" questioned her boyfriend.

"What? You know him??" She replied, in a state of shock.

You see her boyfriend at the time was the valedictorian of Wolfson High School. So in her eyes, a "thug" like me could never have known him, "Yeah... Jizzle, you still going to college next year?"

"Yeah," I answered, eyes locked on Sienna. "I plan to major in entertainment law and business management"

"That sounds good... What are your plans once you obtain a degree?"

"Most likely I'll open up a record label here in Jacksonville."

"Yeah. Well me and Sienna are about to go... I guess I'll see you later." Her boyfriend states, noticing the look I'm giving his woman, but I know he's soft as a piece of tissue in the middle of the Atlantic Ocean.

Later that night, I caught Sienna by herself. "So what's the deal teacher?"

"Will you stop calling me that?" She blushed, "My name is Sienna."

"Oh! Now I can get your name!" I said smiling.

"Listen boy, I am not perfect—"

"That's a matter of opinion." I cut her off.

"I. Make. Mistakes." She continued, seeing the look of want in my eyes.

"Apology accepted. So, when can I take you out?"

"What? Boy, I got a man."

"Naw... You got a boy attempting to become a man."

"Don't talk about Toby like that. He's a good dude."

"Maybe, but why settle for good when you can have the best?"

"Oh, so I guess you're the best!"

44

"On my way to becoming one of them, but enough of the square talk."

"Square talk?"

"Yeah, only square ass niggas feel they have something to prove, I am proof enough."

"Arrogant enough."

"Naw, never that. Never that. Just confident, but here's my number. Call me tomorrow."

"Is that a demand or a request?"

"Ma, if you weren't feeling me in some way, this conversation would've been over... Tomorrow." I said and walked off.

Of course, just as I expected, the next day she called and here we are today. Me standing in the hallway, as my daughter comes running into my arms.

"Sienna, how was your day?"

"The same old... Same old." She said. "I just went to work kind of late today."

"Why?" I asked as if it mattered. Sienna owns her own psychiatric practice. She is the boss.

"Just tired." She answered, in a neutral tone.

"Mmm Hmm, Natasha baby, why don't you go to your room?" Daddy'll be up in a minute to get you ready for your bath." I said, already feeling the argument that is about to start. Once I was sure Natasha is out of eyesight, I turn to my wife.

"So... What's up?"

"What are you talking about Neiros?" She answers. One of them "You know what" kind of looks on her face.

"Listen... I don't have time for the games. Whatever you got going on, just spit the shit out!"

"Okay. Question, where were you at earlier today?"

"What's earlier?" I ask, and to be honest, I know where the conversation is going. One thing about Sienna, she was raised in the streets. The only reason she doesn't know about me trapping is that the only person from around my way that can confirm that I'm funding Gut One is him. Of course, you got those that speculate, but that is a given. Even if I really wasn't in the game.

"Neiros! Don't play with me! Who was with you at Gut One's house when he went to get some medicine for Meka?"

Now, really, I know I'm caught like a muthafucka, but my motto is to deny, deny, and deny! So, I turn around and say

"Nobody" as casually as humanly possible.

Lucky for me, I got this thing about mirrors. Just as I look up, I have time to duck as a big ass glass ashtray comes sailing towards my head.

46

"Whoa! Hold on Si!" I said, with my hands up laughing.

"You think this shit is funny!" She yells, throwing a vase at me.

"Bae! Now that vase cost three hundred dollars!"

"Fuck that vase!" She tosses an equally valuable vase at me.

"Who was that bitch that was with you!"

"Nobody... Just some chick Gut had in the trap. Now, ease up, and let's talk about this." I said, still grinning.

"Talk! Oh, we gone talk about this bitch! Right after I kick yo ass!"

"Damn, I love it when you get ghetto. But Si, you know you can't kick my ass." I said, putting her arms down by her sides.

"Bae, ain't shit happen with her... Just calm yo jealous ass down."

"Neiros, tell me that when it comes to you. I don't have a reason to be jealous."
Now, she had me there. I'd be lying if I said she shouldn't be a little worried about me sliding in some different pussy. One thing I have to give her props on is the that fact, even with all the bullshit I've put this woman through, she still stays with me. I mean the woman came home and caught me in one of our bedrooms with her best friend and cousin. So, the only answer I can give her is a smile.

"Neiros! You fucked that girl didn't you?" She said, tears in her eyes. I don't care what any man says. When your lady is crying about something you did, but you know she can't prove it, it still fucks with you.

The moment that lip goes to trembling, the only thing you can do is exactly what I did. Cover that beautiful ass mouth with my own, "No... Neiros."

She tries to protest; I wasn't hearing that shit though. I just kept walking her backwards until I had her on the bed in one of the rooms on the lower floor. "No," She said, knowing she was saying yes, as I slid them painted on jeans off along her already wet thongs.

Parting her lips with my fingers, she lets out a small gasp once my tongue connects with her dripping honey pot. As much as she wants to be mad at me, the pressure building between her legs forces her to urge me on, as her body arches into my face.

Once she has come twice, I slide into her, commencing to make love to her, holding her in a tight embrace, while slowly pumping in and out of her. Damn, just fucking her. I lightly caress her, stroking with maximum control. This is for her and only her. It's sad to say, but when it comes to giving myself to her, this is the best I can do.
***

After making sure things were straight with Sienna, I go upstairs to talk to one of the only people on this Earth I can say I'm in love with, "Daddy! Was you and mommy fighting?' My inquisitive daughter asks.

"Never that... In order to fight, I would have to hurt your mommy and when you see her, she'll have not one scratch on her."

"Okay." This super-smart seven-year-old says.

"So, how was your day?"

"Good."

"Alright, how was school?"
"Good."

"What's wrong?"

"Nothing."

"Nothing huh," I said, grabbing Natasha and tickling her until she had tears running down her face.
"Okay Daddy! Stop Daddy!".

"Not till you tell me what's wrong."

"Stop tickling me and I'll! I'll! I'll tell you!"

"Alright, spill the beans or I'll be forced to punish you for violating the code of Mr. Tickles."

"I'm sorry Daddy!"
"Daddy! Who is Daddy? I know nothing of this Daddy you speak of!" I said in an English accent.

"I'm sorry Mr. Tickles," Natasha said, with a smile worth more than all the world can offer, "I want a puppy."

"A puppy huh?"

"Yep." She shakes her head up and down, "My friend Carmen has one... So does Tori and Tomika."

"And what kind of puppy do you want?"

"A Rottweiler!"

"A what?"

"Rottweiler Daddy!"

"I don't know..." I said, knowing full well if she wanted a kennel full of Rottweilers, I'd buy them, "Where is it going to sleep?"

"We can get one of them little cute doggy beds."

"Who's going to house train it and walk it?"

"Me... Who else?"

"I'll tell you what," I said, with a grin on my face. "You've got to give me a good reason."

"I'm your little girl!" She says, smiling.

"Naw... You'll still be my little girl with the puppy or not."
"Aww, come on! Daddy, what do I have to do? I'll clean the house." She said, one of those looks that only a little girl can give her father when she wants something. All fathers know

the look, it's that I'm the most innocent person on Earth look.

"You say it... I'll do it."

"Kisses."

"Kisses? How many? One? Two?" She comes toward me lips puckered.

"One hundred."

"One hundred? Daddyy! I can't even count that far yet! I'm only seven!"

"Well, I guess you don't want that puppy." I act like I'm about to get up.

"Daddy! Okay! Okay!" She grabs my arm, "How about fifty?"

"No."

"Seventy-five?" She said while I shake my head, "Boy, you sho make it hard on a little girl."

"Just get to kissing!" I point at my cheek.

"Alright," She said, with a sigh, "Daddy!" She screams when I tackle her and start blowing raspberries on her stomach, "Oh! Oh! You're killing me, daddy!"

"I guess... That's enough for one hundred kisses."

"You slobbered on my stomach!" she exclaimed, wiping her stomach off by rubbing it on my shirt.
"And?"

"Slob is nasty!"

"Even Daddy's?"

"Yep."

"Whatever," I said, getting up to leave.

"Oh... Daddy! This man came by asking about you this morning at school."

"What man and where?"

"At school before I went in the building. When mommy dropped me off."

"What did he say?" I questioned, as all motion on Earth came to a complete and utter stop. It's one thing to fuck with me. Shit, keeping one hundred, you can fuck with my moms, but fuck with Natasha Nichelle Simmons? I promise the only one that'll stop my wrath is God!

"Nothing... He just asked if you were okay, and to tell you he said hello."

"Did he tell you his name?"

"Yep, Diego."

"Mmhmm," I said, trying to appear calm, not to alert my jewel of any danger. Yet at the very moment, Diego doesn't know it, but life, as he knows, has taken a turn for the worst.

As I sit and try to calm my racing pulse, the look on Natasha's face causes me to ask, "What's wrong baby?"

"That." She answers, a little too late and I shift just in time to stop the .762 round from entering my heart, only grazing my arm. The force from the shell still forces me to accelerate backwards a little quicker than I planned, leaving me in a heap on the floor, just as the cellphone rings, "Jizzle" I said, through clenched teeth.

"Please don't think I missed on purpose." says a Spanish accented voice.

"And besides a dead man... Who is this?" I said, steel in my voice.

"Now, why are you asking questions you already know the answer to? Really."

"Diego?"

"None other."

"Well dead man... I'll be seeing you soon. Very soon."

"Well, first you may want to turn around my friend." He tells me.

Following his recommendation, I turn to find Sienna with the barrel of a silenced 9mm pistol to her head.

Cursing myself for leaving my own weapons downstairs after satisfying my wife, I quickly put my other hand in the air, thinking this is a real checkmate move. Life is definitely over.

"Neiros." Diego says, arrogance dripping off my name as he speaks it, "I need you to understand something. As you can see, I've got the upper hand in this situation, but..." he pauses, to add emphasis to his words, "For me to kill you, that would be a grave mistake. For you are more valuable alive than dead."

"Is that so?" I reply, honestly confused. Ain't no way in hell I would have my enemy in this type of situation, after invading his home and allowing him to still breathe once I'm gone!

"Yes, that is so. This is just a display of power, shall we say. The powerful are not just solidified by his physical strength, but more so by his intellectual strength. This is the conclusion of this episode. I know enough about you to wipe your very existence from the face of the Earth. From beginning to end! All I want is a 50/50 split of both False Reality Records and all of your dope houses in this city."
Is this pancho crazy! There's no way I'm going to split my life with him, just on the premise of him catching me slipping one time! One thing Hunter taught me though, if you stroke the ego of the powerful, their power soon will become their weakness.

"I must admit Diego, I did underestimate your reach. But I am going to need some time to think this over."

"Time?"

"Yeah. It isn't often I'm put in such situations. I've always prided myself on being one step ahead of any situation, yet... here I am outsmarted and outdone."

"24 hours. That's all you get."

"Plenty," I said, knowing full well he just fucked up. Even if he does have some surveillance on me, in 24 hours, it won't even matter."

Feeling a lot better about the situation, I relax as one of his goons receives a text message.

"Now, now," he says in my ear, "I know you didn't think I would make it that easy for you... Huh?"

He states, as two more men enter the room, picking my daughter up, "Daaddy!" My jewel screams, instant tears falling down her angelic face, grasping my heart in the process.

"If you so much as invite the thought to harm—"

"Yeah, yeah! All you have to do is comply... 24 hours!" He demands, then the phone goes dead, the silence on the other end tricking my mind into thinking I hear his voice echoing. "Neiros!" shouts Sienna, bringing me back to this weird.

Looking at the cell phone in my hand. I realize a total of six minutes and twenty-four seconds has passed.

"Baby! Are you okay?" She continues, placing my face in her hands.

"What the fuck kind of question is that!" I snap, knowing she means well, yet unable to control my anger.

"Neiros! Why did they take my baby?" She questions, with a look in her eyes that I've had yet to see in them. It's a look I've only seen in the eyes of a killer. That calm, yet detached look. It must be that motherly instinct coming to frustration.

"Tell me the truth." She says, so calm that it's scary.

"Bae, they want 50% of the label," I say, only giving her a half-truth.

"The label... This is about the label!" She said, with a hint of skepticism in her voice.

"Yes," I replied, still in my zone. One thing I know, at this point, I'm all in. "Yeah," I state as my cellphone rings.

"It's a shame you are slipping so bad... So easily caught off guard." A familiar, yet impossible voice says.

"Who is this?" My heart races.

"Has it been that long? You've really forgotten how my voice sounds."

"Listen, I ain't got time for games!"
"Life is a game... Have you become a pawn? If that's the case, it's not shocking that you have ended up in this situation."

"Hmm," I state, my pulse steadily picking up.

"So tell me Neiros, in the world full of men, this world full of mortals... When did you cease to stop thinking like a God and start taking actions based on the wants of your flesh?" Hunter said, proving my assumption right.

"Hunter? But, but...how?"

"Why question someone in which you know thinks with immortal sense."

Chapter 4

Bismillahir-Rahmanir Rahim. Alhamado Lillah Rabbil Alameen." recites Hamzah, as he completes the Asr prayer Muslims are obligated to perform, as part of their five obligatory prayers.

After completion of his last prostration and reciting the Tashahud, a supplication for a blessing upon the Prophet Muhammad, as Allah blessed his friend Abraham.

Hamzah Taslims out of the prayer, standing to his feet feeling more at ease than he was prior to the salat.

Walking his 6'2" frame over to the mirror, he runs a comb through his beard that hangs down to his massive chest, shaking his shoulder-length dreads. He looks into his deep black eyes, taking in his African features, from his wide nose to his big lips, and knows why his purplish-black skin is the color it is.

Hamzah got his name from one of the early reverts to Islam and the Prophet Muhammad's uncle. Being that Hamzah was a warrior, it was only right that this street warrior takes his name.

Hamzah was enlisted in the military, where he did a couple of tours in Afghanistan. The exposure to Islam piqued his interest and upon being discharged, he started studying. Soon he reverted to Islam with the intent of living a life of righteousness.

Months of searching for a job, made him to realize that the only real skill he possessed was that of being a killer. Then one day, down on his luck, out of money, a big-time dealer offered him twenty grand to eliminate his competition. Hamzah did such an efficient job. The dealer started to recommend him to his friends. The rest is history. For Hamzah, his profession is just that. His goal is to be placed in a position to only practice his way of life. He knows he must ask Allah for forgiveness with each prayer he does because there is no telling when some unsuspecting hustler will fall victim to his guns. So he constantly prays for forgiveness and makes a duo for Allah to give him a way out of the streets.

"Hello," He says, into his iPhone.

"Hamzah."

"Jizzle...long time no hear."

"Well, you know me, if I call..."

"It's about money. How much Allah?"

"A cool million."

"A million dollars! Jizzle, stop bullshittin!" exclaims Hamzah, and only gets silence as an answer. "Who has to die?"

"A lot of muthafuckas. You in?"

"A million dollars? Yeah!"

"Alright, I'll be in touch."

"Irisha Allah," Hamzah said, disconnecting.

I sat at my desk, finger in a steeple, thinking about the events of the last two hours. After my unsuspecting phone call from Hunter, I decided to call Diego and tell him I would agree to his terms. I guess the muthafucka is craftier than I thought. He still decided to keep Natasha as a form of insurance. I guess to keep me in line, but I promise, he'll be dead...and soon.

The next thing is to really analyze this Hunter situation. As he said, he thinks with what he calls Immortal sense. The thing is, Hunter doesn't see himself as a deity of any kind. What this statement means is this: Hunter believes that preordainment is the ultimate form of wisdom. The creator has everything written out, down to the last second of everyone's life on Earth. Being that we can't predict our last day, short of suicide. Which is a coward's way out in His eyes. He feels that in order to be as close to supreme as one can get. You must mimic the One who created you.

Thus, one must know every detail of one's day down to the best of his human ability. With the thought that man can't control the actions of his fellow man, yet he can control what happens in his arena. Short of causes outside of his control, i.e. accidents, natural disasters, etc.

Hunter doesn't compromise at all! This is the only man I've ever met, that writes out every day of his life months ahead of time. Each day has what he calls variables, that just in case something out of his control happens, other things go into effect.

That is why I thought he was dead, I buried him. You don't get it. I saw his body, or a likeness of his body, go into the ground. One thing I didn't do...

I pulled out a small box that was a gift given to me at the time of his death. Opening the box, I find a piece of cloth that read-
...and because of their sayings, we killed Messiah, son of Maryam. The message of Allah. But they killed him not, nor crucified him, but the resemblance of Isa was put over another man, and those who differ therein are full of doubts. They have no certain knowledge, they follow nothing but conjecture, for surely; they killed him not. Quran 4:157

Folding the cloth up, I think to myself, the sad part... Hunter knew I wouldn't open the box. That's just the type of man he is. His knowledge of a person's actions is uncanny and almost creepy. I get chills just thinking about it.

Why is he back? More importantly, why did he fake his death, to begin with?

"Edward." Life said, into a cellphone.

"Salutations!"
"Are you any closer to finding out who Death is?"
"Well, actually, I'm close. But something tells me this is only a picture of him in disguise. Check your messages."

Life checks the messages on the phone and finds a picture of Death in disguise. "Well Ed, thank you. It's a start."

"Jizzle," Tivia said, walking her fine ass into my office. "I'm going to be out of town for about a week or two. I got with

61

the staff and put things in order. So, the only thing you'll have to do is go over the paperwork and sign it." She said, and bent over that fat ass sticking up in the air, even with all the bullshit going on around here, I can't help but think about fucking the shit out of Tivia. Acting on my desires, I get up, walk over to her, pushing my erection up against that soft ass.

"Jizzle, what are you doing?"
"Tivia," I respond, voice thick with lust. "Stop the bullshit. You know you want this dick."

"But—"

"But what?" I said, pulling her now unbuttoned Gucci jeans down, marveling at them pretty ass thigs, damn this bitch fine!

"Sienna?"

"Fuck that! Man tighten up" I step back watching Tivia comply. Noticing once she lifts her shirt up, she ain't got on no panties!

My soulja almost bust out of my designer jeans as Tivia gives me one of them pre-fuck faces, turns around, grabbing a chair, bending over. Then looks back, a wisp of golden-brown hair falling over one eye.

"I've waited for this moment for a minute... Don't disappoint." Then makes her ass jump while she distances her feet.

What? Don't disappoint? She got Jizzle fucked up. I do this! I said to myself into mash mode, aggressively grabbing Tivia by the waist, slamming into her wet box like I'm mad as fuck.

"Oh... Aye Papi!" She practically chants, saying some other Spanish shit, throwing that ass back causing waves to ripple them cheeks like a violent ocean. The sight of the cheeks and the sound of the wetness only sent me into murder mode.

Totally into this shit, I scoop her sexy ass up, slamming her on my desk, sending paper flying everywhere. Pulling her to me, I continue to pound into that wet box with relentless force. The sound of skin slapping, Tivia moaning sentences in Spanish, almost pushing me over the edge. Yet, I've been doing this since I was eleven. So I got mad dick control. Slowing my thrust, I flip Tivia onto her stomach, bending her legs up, pounding into her with long-medium speed strokes. She is a pitch from screaming, as she informs me this is her third nut.

With one last thrust, I pull out of her, looking in amazement as she quickly gets on her knees, swallowing me completely. As all of the energy in my body shoots down her throat, I grab the back of her head, throwing my head back, just as the door opens.

Looking over my shoulder, I see Sienna standing at the door with her cellphone clutched to her chest, tears running down her face. But this nut is so damn good, all I can do is allow my knees to give out and fall. Only to turn my head, finding the door empty, and Sienna gone.

Chapter 5

I convinced Tivia to go at it a second time, which took all of about five seconds. The way I saw it, we'd been caught, so why stop?

I sat and thought about the fix I am in with Sienna. Honestly, the last thing I need is this bullshit, yet it is the way it is. Boy, they weren't lying when they said, when it rains, it pours!

"What Neiros!" Snaps Sienna.

"Listen, I am not about to sit here and start with the I'm sorry shit. You caught me in the middle...well, end. The only thing I can ask is, where do we go from this point on?"

"WE? Are you fucking serious! After I catch you fucking this bitch? You still think there is a we?"

Now, at this point, with all the bullshit going on, I'm really, truly not in the mood for the shit. And she's making it too easy to end this, but on the strength of my daughter...

"Sienna, before you do something you may regret later, think about it this way. You can't tell me for one second, you really thought, with the life I live, I was being 100% faithful to you?"

"That's always been the problem. I knew you was cheating, and I just ate it up. Praying one day that you'd just stop."

"Okay. Now bae, I'm not saying that day will not come, it will, but, I ain't gone lie, I'm addicted to pussy."

"Then why don't you just come home? What? I don't give you enough?"

"It ain't you. It...ain't you. Pussy for me is like candy."

"Candy."

"Yeah, candy. You know how a kid was locked in a candy shop would have to try each and every piece."

"Mmm... Hmm." She said, clearly not feeling this shit.

"Well, Jacksonville is my candy shop... Pussy is my candy."

"That's your excuse?"

"Bae, that ain't an excuse. It's the truth! I'm fucked up!"

"You're fucked up. Then get some help."

"The only one that can help me, is me."

"So what's stopping you?"

"Honestly, just not ready to stop."

"You can't be serious!"

"Listen... If you want lies, I can't do it."

"Well, when you can... You know what Neiros? Fuck you! How about that? Fuck you!" She yells, hanging the phone up.

Listening to the silence on the other end, I know I should feel bad. I mean my wife just pretty much broke up with me.

To be honest though, the timing could not have been any better. Because now, I can just live as Death.

Once she got dressed, Tivia left False Reality Records with her juice box still dripping. She has wanted Jizzle since the first moment she met him for an interview.

"So," Jizzle said, sizing Tivia up. "I see you've got the education to work for me but tell me a lil something about your upbringing."

"Well," She started, taking in the way he fit just right into his outfit. His well-defined muscles accentuated the fact that he worked out. She could tell that he was turned on by her. The imprint on his thigh as he sat on his desk with one leg on the ground, he took measures to hide was a clear sign of that. "I was born in Columbia, raised in Brooklyn, I really don't know—"

"Columbia and Brooklyn, huh?" He cut her off, "So you know a lil something about the streets?"

"You could say that."

"Good, listen... I do not plan on having some soft ass female up in here, that's all timid and shit. If you have a problem with muthafuckas telling you the truth, or your feelings get hurt easily, this is not the spot for ya."

"Oh... Well" She said slightly taken aback by his blunt honesty, "I'm tough enough."
"Really?" He smirks, "What color thongs you got on?"

"Excuse me!"

66

"Bitch, I ain't stutter! What color thongs you got on!"

"Sky, sky blue."

"Let me see them shits." He demanded.

"Uh, Mr.Simmons..."

"Jizzle."

"Well, Jizzle. What does my underwear have to do with this job?"

"Everything, take them jeans off."

With a bit of hesitation, Tivia started to unbutton her jeans. Truth be told, if Neiros wanted the pussy, he could've had it at the precise moment.

"Damn!" He exclaimed. "That pussy fat as a muthafucka! Let me see that bitch."

Tivia must've said fuck it to herself because she pulled down her sky-blue thongs, sitting in the chair, legs wide open.

"That's what the fuck I'm talking about, keep this shit Tivia. This isn't something I do at all. I just had a gut feeling about you. I run a company and conduct business in different ways. I need people like you, a lot of muthafuckas say they can take a lot of shit. They tough, all that fly shit. But you just proved two things to me: you're confident in your body and willing to take the risk and you trust me to some degree or have a good judge of character. You ain't know if I was some perverted ass muthafucka or what, yet you just bust your legs open for a nigga. A woman confident in her body is confident in herself, and therefore the opinions of others don't matter to her. She knows where she stands and her worth. I also need risk-takers. So you're hired, put that shit back on before I fuck the shit out of ya ass."

Coming back to the present, she sits in her car, smiling to herself, as tremors from the thought of Jizzle inside her still run through her mind. One thing she is certain of is if Sienna doesn't want him, she has no problem filling in the void. Pulling out of the underground garage, Tivia drives cautiously towards her home. One thing she knows about her bother is never underestimate him.

With that in mind, she formulates a plot to build an army big enough to take him down, but what then? Being truthful with herself, she knows she doesn't want to run her family's business, yet she can't allow Temera to completely take over either. He'll cause a war that may destroy her entire family.

All of her thoughts are put on hold, as she takes notice of a red Lexus that makes the same turn she does. To make sure she isn't tripping, she makes another turn, only to see the same
car, a couple of seconds later. Knowing that if she can just get home. She'll be okay, she speeds up to get there faster.

"It's about time." A once childhood friend says, sitting on her sofa, with legs crossed, a bottle of Aquafina in his hand. "Miguel." She states, hand in the air, closing the door behind her.

Miguel Juarbe stares in her eyes while standing to his full height of 5'4", walks over to her with a smile that comes friendly, yet sinister in the same token.

"Well..." He runs his hand through his medium-length black hair, "It seems as if your sibling is starting to become a thorn in my side... and Tivia, I hate thorns!" He states, dropping his chin slightly, giving her a look void of any friendliness. "So, what does that have to do with me?"

"Everything... You see, I know you are the only person your brother really loves. So, kidnap you... Uhhh," He waves his hands, "bring him out, kill you both. No more thorns... You got me?"

"Bravo... Bravo!" She claps, with a blank expression on her face, "Brilliant plan genius, but one problem." Her finger comes up.

"And that would be?"

"My brother wants me dead."

"Oh, I know that... But," He mimics her by raising his finger. "The enemy of my enemy is my friend... In layman's terms. Yes, your brother and you are having family problems, yet me kidnapping you... He'll put those petty differences aside, become friends, and attempt to get me out of the way."

"You definitely mustn't know Temero very well!"

"on the contrary... I know this, the only reason your brother is at war with you, is only due to your attitude, not his. Plus,

69

he'll most definitely want the honor of killing you, versus me doing so." He smiles.

"And... You really believe that." She smirks, knowing full well that Miguel's statement is based on conjecture, with not an ounce of certain knowledge to stand on.

Once Temero decided to crossover, there wasn't an ounce of thought towards self-vengeance. Only self-preservation."

"Listen Miguel, I'm going to be completely honest with you... Temero doesn't give two fucks about how I die. If he does it or not. To him, dead is dead... Now if you want him out of the way, I have a proposition for you."

At the mention of the word proposition, Miguel peeked up like a small dog that sees a treat in the hands of its master, "I'm all ears."

"You and I team up, and eradicate Temero." She throws out in the air, watching the wheels in Miguel's head turn.

"Now, my sweet, sweet Tivia... What's in it for me?"

"Honestly Miguel, I do not want any part of the drug trade... Yet, I would not mind profiting from it."

"What's the split?" He said, greed in his eyes.

"70, 30."

"Now, why would I take such a small percentage and do all the work?"

"Oh, you'll get the 70%."

"Are you serious?"

"Yes." Tivia beams, knowing she has Miguel where she wants him.

"And how will your family feel about this... Uh, arrangement?"

"Honestly, If I know Temero, the only person left alive to protest is him and mother... Whom at this time is more than likely in bondage by him."
"Well Tivia, since you put it so elegantly, how could I refuse such an offer?" He smiles.

"Good." Tivia takes a breath, "So let's—"

"But," Miguel cuts her off, the smile all but gone from his face, "only a fool would even take the chance of getting bit by a snake..."

"Miguel!"

"Miguel nothing! Tie her—"

Miguel is cut short as the door burst open, the shell from a silenced 9mm into one of the two henchmen. Instinct kicking in, Tivia swiftly rolls out of the way, scrambling for her sofa where she keeps a .45 hidden for such situations, as lead continues to fly. Putting one hand on the pistol, she hears a feminine voice say, "Tivia! Really it's not that serious!" Looking up, gasping for air, she finds the face of her college friend staring down at her with a warm smile plastered on her face. "Akema! When the hell did you get in town!"

"Girlll! I've been in town for about a month," states Akema, giving Tivia a hand up from the floor.

"How did you know shit was going down?

"I was following you earlier."

"Red Lexus?"

"Yep."

"Damn, that was sloppy!"
"Bitch! I wasn't trying to hide, but once I saw you rush into your house and stop the way you did... I knew something was wrong."

"Well, bet that shit up!" Tivia looks into Akema's eyes reminiscing about how they met.

"Oh! Excuse me!" A young Tivia said, coming out of the library on the campus of the University of California.

"No, that was all me." Akema bends down helping her with her books. "I should have been watching where I was going."

"Same here."

"Well, since I almost knocked you down... How about lunch?" "Sure," Tivia responded, feeling timid around Akema, not yet understanding why.

As months passed, Tivia and Akema became the best of friends. To the point where they decided to move in with each other. For Tivia, this was the first time she'd been this close to any female outside her family. Yet with Akema, it was as if she could be more than just herself. It seemed as if Akema brought the best out of her, character-wise. Exposing hidden qualities and traits she didn't even know existed.

"Tivia! What's wrong?" Akema exclaims, in the middle of the first semester as Tivia comes slamming into their lush apartment. "Tell me! What's the matter?" She demands, sitting down on Tivia's big, expensive bed.

If someone came and looked inside their abode, they would swear the two women were the children of millionaires. Just a quick glance into their living room would bring them to this conclusion. This was all paid for by Tivia's relatives. From the three 52" flat screen T.V., the complete computer setups for both Tivia and Akema, all the way to the $2500 rent that's been paid for their entire stay in college. Akema tried to insist she be allowed to pull her own weight, yet Tivia insisted her friendship was weight enough.

"Angelo broke up with me!" Tivia screams, through tears, pounding her thighs with her fists.

"He broke up with you! How the fuck?"

"He said... he said..." she sniffs, "he was tired of fucking sophomores and wanted some senior pussy!"

"He said what?" Said Akema, a low rumble in her words. If there was one thing she didn't tolerate, it was disrespect towards the few friends she had. At that moment she set in her mind that she was definitely going to pay Angelo a visit, but first, she had to console her crying friend.

Akema started to wipe the tears away from Tivia's face all the while giving her assurance that everything would be O.K. Just the sign of Tivia's puffy eyes and said expression made Akma's heart ache, but it also did something else she had yet to share with Tivia.

Going on emotion alone, she learns in and kisses Tivia lightly on the lips. The shocked expression on her best friend's face almost made her regret her actions, but her lower region was so wet, she could feel the moisture of her panties, clinging to her body.

"Akema! What are you doing?" Tivia gasps, in verbal protestation, yet physically she was not stopping Akema as she started to suck on her neck while massaging her breast. "Akema, I... We." She starts to say, deciding to moan as Akema works magic with her tongue, lightly running it around her erect nipples. All the while inserting two fingers inside of Tivia's soaking wet, working them in and out in a circular motion, pulling her in front of her between her legs in order to use her other hand's thumb and forefinger to stimulate her clitoris.

"Akema, please, please don't stop." Tivia pleads, grabbing Akema's hair, riding her finger, moaning as her best friend sends feelings through her body no man has ever taken the time to produce.

Tivia almost loses her mind as she's laid on her back, kisses caressing her stomach like Akema's lips are an intimate lover alone. Before she can react, a breath escapes her mouth once Akema takes her pulsating clit into her mouth, still fingering her. Then sucking and licking, her finger hooked inside, still moving. Within minutes, Tivia's juices flow opening up an ocean of sensations throughout her body. As they flow unrestrained into Akema's throat, the best orgasm Tivia's ever had in her twenty years on Earth assaults her body.

After the two women go at each other until the early morning hours, Akema the teacher, Tivia the willing pupil. They end up in bed with satisfied smiles that not even money can buy.

"Well..." Akema said, bringing Tivia back into the present,

"We need to get rid of this mess, so I can get me some of that pussy."

"Yeah," Tivia whispered in a low growl, jeans soaked from the memories. "But first, what the fuck is this!"

"A long story!"

"Baby... I ain't going no where, so we got all night."

Chapter 6

L ife sits on a sofa on the phone with Edward discussing some of the details of the hit to be pulled on Death by Life. In thought, the irony of the situation was funny, the most feared hitmen in the game coined themselves Life and Death.

That has to be one crazy-ass coincidence. But truthfully, Life knows completing this hit isn't something that is going to be completed with ease. This was no average mark.

"So, tell me... How do you plan to pull this off?" Asks Edward.

"Honestly Ed, the more I sit and contemplate this hit, the more I realize it is going to be more difficult than I first thought."

"Well, it's definitely well worth the effort, Life."

"Question... How much time do the contractors give me before the deal is off the table?"

"You see, that is the most perplexing thing... There is no special amount of time you must complete the hit. And to my understanding, they must have some way of keeping tabs on you, because they also plan to increase the amount after each failed attempt.

"How much?"

"10% of the starting amount."

"Woah, oh, oh! Listen Ed! Who the fuck are these people!"

"Perfectly honest... I have the slightest idea. I met with a lawyer from a firm that is virtually non-existent as far as my research has revealed. And he just pops out of the fucking blue like some sort of ghost or something" Edward thought back to his first encounter with Tavis Teams...

Edward had just returned from the gun range trying out some R.I.P. rounds he'd purchased, walking inside of his five-bedroom, two-bath home in Ponte Vedro.

Flicking the light switch, he immediately draws his firearm, realizing his power has been cut.

Creeping slowly, in a mid-crouch he was taught in training camp. Edward eases around the corner, pistol first, stopping the moment he sees a shadowy figure sitting on the sofa in his living room, both of his well-trained Dobermans by its side. Totally baffled, Edward keeps his gun trained on the figure, certain that his dogs should have ripped this man apart. The fact that they haven't only piqued his curiosity as to who is seated on his couch.

"Hello Edward." the figure says, in a calm voice. "You may be wondering why your puppies haven't attempted to tear me limb from bloody limb. But oh... They tried. Let's just say dogs are a lot like children. After hours of play, they just give up." He throughs his hands up. "Don't be upset with them...
I've trained for better mutts than they'll ever be."

"And you are?"

"Tavis. Tavis Teams... Head attorney employed by the R.M. Group."

"The R.M. Group?"
"Yeah... They have rather, umm... What would be a fitting term? Ah!" He snaps his fingers, "Lucrative... Yeah, lucrative proposition for you and your associate."

"Me and my associate?"

"Yes, you, and Life... Come on now Ed." He said, seeing the attempt at a confused look on Edward's face, "Let's not do the whole play stupid role, please... Evidently, I'm of the knowledge of your association with Life. So, let's cut the bullshit, shall we? My employers are willing to offer five million dollars for the body of Death. Dead of course." He steeples his fingers awaiting a response.

"Five million dollars?"

"Yes... A group of about ten to fifteen investors has come together and these are their teams." He said, pulling an envelope from the inside of his suit jacket, "A contact number is in the envelope."

"How long do I have to give an answer?"

"At your convenience, absolutely no rush," Tavis said, walking out of the front door. Edward rushes outside, only to find nature, no sign of Tavis Teams or a get-away vehicle...

"That sounds like some sort of horror movie." Life said, after hearing the details of Edward's meeting.

"Yeah... But I'll try and find out who our man is—"

"No Need." Life said.

"No need?" Ed comes up short.

"Yeah... Death's real name is Neiros Simmons." "You're talking about the C.E.O. of False Reality Records, Neiros Simmons?"

"The one and only."

"If you don't mind me asking, how the fuck do you know this for sure?"

"The ring."

"The... Rings?"

"Yes, Ed... The ring. It's the same one I gave him on our 1st Anniversary." Sienna said, "It's engraved till death do us part or life takes its course."

It's been two days since the shit with Sienna went down, but that doesn't mean that money doesn't need to be made. Yeah, I got a lot on my plate, yet a soulja doesn't fold under pressure. He stands up and handles business.

In my office, I sit behind my desk contemplating my next move. I still have to sit down with Hamzah and some more soldiers I hit up, but that's a given.

Oh! Did I mention Gut One going through some street beef shit with some cats out in the Sherwood? Yeah, peep this shit. How about this nigga in the club with one of his niggas when they get into a fight with some other niggas over a chick Gut One is fucking. Well, Gut One and his nigga beat the shit out the niggas, yet I'm sure as you know, in the streets, pride is a muthafucka and even in death, vengeance still lives. "Yo! Jizzle! What's up brah!" said Murder, walking into my office. Keeping it one hundred, this muthafucka turned out to be more real than a lot of niggas that I know. I mean this white boy on some real get-money shit. His honesty and loyalty are hard to match. "Murder boy, what's the business?"

"I got this mixtape shit I wanted to run by you real quick." He said, putting a C.D. in my system.

As soon as the beat comes in, I can tell he had Simple, our beat technician hook this shit up. One thing about Simp, he got a distinct sound to his music. Murder comes in and blows me away:
I'm on John Wayne shit, bitch I got Six shooter / Oriental bitch 4'6" with a big rugger / Get slick real shit, let the bitch do ya / Fuck ya till ya sick spit six through ya / That's how I move pimp, smoother than an ocean's breeze / Ego sitting higher than eagle blowing tons of trees / Get it... My life is a bitch / Pick her up on main had her turning tricks on 28th / That's when the kid learn, boy you got a gift / Cuz I was fucking Destiny and the game by 26 / At 27 scooped wisdom, ignorance wasn't with / Now it's safe to say I'll be the shit by 30...

Damn! This cracka snapping on this bitch! I guess I'm going to have to tell my other artist to step their shit up. Murder might be the next best contender bullshitting, "So, how does that shit sound to you?" He asked.

"Listen, this is what I want... You, Mac, Young Terror, and E.Z. on a False Reality Compilation."

"Yo, I'm all for that Jizzle. But them dudes be on some real busta ass shit! Yo, I understand the whole me being a white boy shit. I ain't sweating that shit. Hell, I ain't really running with a lot of white boys myself, but I did a background on dem dudes. Yeah, they get it in a lil bit, but man... I'm really slumping shit, ya feel me! Except for Mac and he ain't on that murder shit like I am, them other cats just some dope bodies hunting to shine shit."

I smile. Day to day this white boy shows me being real has nothing to do with your skin. Granted, I knew that, but it's always good to see it live. "You know what, you just said some real ass shit... This is the bottom line though, I run this shit. So if I told them niggas to do a song with Elton John, standing butt naked on top of his piano with a pink bow tie on, they got two choices. Either do it or find themselves another label... So, if they so much as give you a fucked-up look, let me know."

"Yo, I ain't on that snitching shit!"

"I feel you... Neither am I. here's the problem with the youth of today though, you can't say you ain't on some shit, but can't truly define what you say you ain't on! I got a business to run. This ain't some hard operation. I got a business to run. So fuck a nigga's feeling or any of that shit. If a muthafucka feel he ain't got to abide by the laws Jizzle set up in my shit, he got me fucked up!"

"What? You'll just fire his ass?"

81

"Now homie, that shit too easy. Plus it isn't enough. Question, what does God do to those who defy Him?"

"Send their asses to hell."

"Exactly! So, I have my own version of hell."

"And that is?"

"Hmm! Just hope you never have to find out." "That's what it do." He shrugs my comment off like it's nothing, "On some other shit, you fuck with that dude Gut One?"

"Why?"

"Listen, I'm asking a question I already know the answer to. Just watch buddy. He ain't on some real shit."

"As in?"

"You support that dude?"

"Why?" I ask, wondering where this line of questioning is coming from, "And how do you know I fuck with him?"

"I cop from dude and overheard him talking to some chick about how you was his nigga and can set a meeting up."

"Mmm Hmm," I said, knowing that sounded like some shit Gut One would say. One thing about brah, he'll use a nigga's name to get up in a bitch, but this muthafucka got my full attention now.

One lesson prison has taught me, a lot of muthafuckas love lip service. Yeah, that shit seems good when it comes out of the mouth, but their actions in your presence and away proves they just attempting to sound cool. It's all a lot of times just bullshit. The truth, everybody wants to be successful, but everybody ain't Drake. So they'll say whatever it takes to sound successful.

I got mad love for Gu One, but as I said, it's one thing to say what you'll do just because the time presents itself and someone you feel is going to believe the bullshit you saying is going for. It's a whole other thing to use lip service without thinking about the consequences. Niggas get robbed and killed based on the same principles daily. So these things I'm hearing about my nigga ain't shocking, due to how I see life. I've already explained how I trust my niggas. "So why would I have a reason to worry?"

"Listen Jizzle, you sound like you're getting mad about this shit."

"Not in the least. Even the ones you love have a period where the decisions they make can cause you to distrust them."

"True, very true. This is how I see it, you're a businessman. The last thing you need is somebody out here spreading rumors and connecting you to the stretch, ya feel me? Dude got a very loose tongue."

That's all he's talking about! Here I am about to go into kill mode, and he's just talking about Gut One's flamboyant tongue!

Some of you so-called "real" niggas are most likely like I'm a "real" fuck nigga for doubting my nigga. If that's your stance, peep this shit. In the dictionary, the definition of "real" is being or occurring to fact or actuality, not imaginary or ideal 2. genuine; not artificial.

So, if you want to call yourself "real", look at the title you're placing upon yourself. So if you cross that line for being "real", which is "real" easy, due to the fact that the definition of "real" can cause you to get punished for being "real".

So if my nigga, brother, bitch, I don't give a fuck who, did something that was "Real," I'm going to punish them. The reason being is even if Gut One did some flaw that's a "real" flaw. It's a fact that brings on other facts, but just to sum this up, it's impossible for a human being to not be real.

Me, I'm true. True to myself, true to my values, true to my family. I was born real. My life is a reality. One of many, yet a reality nonetheless. "Listen Murder, I really appreciate your concern," I said with a smile. "But Gut One is my brother. To be honest, if you hadn't explained yourself, I was going to peel your whole top off for instigating something flaw about my brother."

"I would expect nothing less." Murder said, getting up to leave.

"But sincerely, bet that up," I said as the phone on my desk rang. "What's up Tiffany?"

"Your friends are waiting in the conference room."

"Bet that up and ummm... Take the rest of the day off."

"Thank you Jizzle." She said, in one of the sexiest tones a woman can have. Shit, now that me and Sienna aren't together, I might as well bust Tiffany's little petite, sexy ass up too... Hey, I told y'all I'm fucked up!

Walking down the hallway, I change my persona. It's time to get in murder mode. I think to myself as I open the door and see my three-man hit squad. "As-salamu. Alaykum." I greet Hamzah.

"Jizzle" He shakes his head, "You're not Muslim."

"So?"

"So, that means you haven't the slighting idea what you're saying or how dear it is to a Muslim, you don't think for a second I'm offended... I'm not."

"Enlighten me."
"Maybe later... Right now, we're here about something I'm going to have to repent to Allah about."

"True." I agree, turning to the other two men in the room,

"Kane. Neo..."
Kane is a Puerto Rican male standing 6'1", with the body of the Rock. Looking into his brown eyes, it sometimes seems as if all life is gone and all that is left in an empty shell, yet he gets the job done. Kane has a black belt in Shotokan, he is also a master in Akido, Jujitsu, Jeet kune do, and Tichi.

The man's father started him killing on the pathways in Puerto Rico at the age of ten, yet Kane is a bad dream compared to Neo.

This 6'7" Caucasian is a walking nightmare. Neo has the whole serial killer thing down to a science. Listening to some of his murders and even people like Kane tell him to ease up. Plus, you've seen what I'm capable of, Neo gives me the creeps.

"Neiros, who's the victim... Or victims?" Neo said, putting added emphasis on his last word, eyes lighting up at the thought of mass murder.

"This Pancho by the name of Diego."

"He must be well protected for you to call us."

"Umm, yeah... and no. Peep this fellow. I'm willing to pay all of you a million each. The thing is, you have to eradicate Diego's entire family."

"That's it!" Hamzah states. "Allahu Akber... With this, I can finally get out of this life so displeasing to my Lord!"

"Hamzah... Kids and all."

"Hey, I'll leave that part to the soulless brothers beside me."

"When do we start?" Asked Kane, smiling at Hamzah's statement.

"Once I talk to him about getting my daughter back."

"He has Natasha? I could retrieve her for you." Offers Hamzah.

"Naw, don't want to alert him—" I hold my finger up as my phone rings, "Yeah, Sienna what's up?"

"I need you to come home."

"For?"

"So we can discuss the terms of our split."

"That shit can wait."

"No Death, it won't."

"What did you call me?!" I stand up, my heart starting to pound in my chest, my body heading up.

"Your name... Death." Sienna said, totally taking me for a loop. That's the last name on this planet Sienna should be calling me. "What! The cat got your tongue?" She said, and I can feel the smirk on her face through the phone, "Let me guess, your life of different faces is finally coming face to face."

"Give me about thirty."

"Thought you'd see it my way." She hangs the phone up.

"Man," Hamzah says, "You look like you've just got off the phone with a ghost."

"You know what Hamzah... I might've just had."

Chapter 7

In Callahan, Florida, just on the outskirts of Jacksonville, Diego sits in his almost fortress. It's been going on two weeks since his last contact with Neiros has started. He already knows a man like Neiros is not going to take this deal laying down. So it's only a matter of time before he attempts to eliminate him.

"Hello," Diego said, to a lovely gentleman by the name of Mike Wallis, as he walks into his office door. "You said you have some valuable information about Mr. Simmons that can possibly help me. So?"

"Well," Mike says, with a swing of his long dreads and smile inviting one to trust him, yet warning one to keep a safe distance all in the same manner. "It seems Jizzle has formed a hit squad of some of the best killers living in the city of Jacksonville. And if my intel is correct, they should be meeting or have met at this very moment."

"Hmmm" Diego spins in his chair, "A hit squad you say. "Well, none of that matters... I have his daughter." He laughs.

"Trust me," Mike said, pulling a Cuban cigar out of his break pocket, clipping the end, letting the discarded portion fall on Diego's plush carpet. "That little tidbit of leeway will end before you know it."

"Clean that shit up!" Diego snaps, leaning forward on his desk.

"Now, why would I do that?" Mike puts fire to the end of his expensive cigar, puffing, blowing smoke in Diego's face.

"Evidently Sir... You have the slightest idea who you're fucking with!" Diego shoots Mike a wicked grin. "Now, this is my last time... Clean that shit up, before I make you do it with your mouth."

"Entertain me shall you." Mike grins, dismissing Diego's statement, "Let's sightsee."

"What?"

"Let's walk the grounds."

"Not before—"

"I'll get it when we return." He waves Diego off, "Like I said... Entertain me."

Going along with this insane man's request, Diego comes from behind his desk, accompanying Mike out of his office, into the living room. From the first look, Diego feels something isn't right. As soon as they walk out the front door, his suspicions are confirmed.

Diego's heart drops from his chest to his feet, as the front door opens, and he's greeted by five masked men, all of them armed with silenced assault rifles. With red beams pointing in the same spot, Diego's heart.

Thinking he's in some sort of warped dream, his knees get weak at the sight of his twenty-guard security team neatly arranged in his yard to spell: Gotcha!!

"Meet seal team seven," Mike said, with a bright smile. "Hey, hey." Hey pats Diego on the back, "Diego, my man... You sure look like you could use some sun. Kind of pale there buddy, don't worry. It's not your time to go just yet. As you can see, each one of the bodies has a stack of cash on it. $100,000 to be exact. Just a little something to make this war interesting. So... I'll be taking Natasha, hopefully you'll start building..." Mike waves his hands, "...Something, adios!"

Diego stands in his yard hotter than a kilo of cocaine in the bag of a janitor, in the police memorial building. He watches ass Mike and the seal team leave as quietly as they seem to have appeared. "This muthafucka think it's just going to be that easy to take me out!" Diego yells into the air.

"Stevo." A man answers on the other end of the line.

"Stevo... Diego."

"Hey! Long time my friend! What brings this call about?" I need to speak to the mole."

"Whoa! El Mole! You sure about that?"

"One hundred percent."

"Two days."

"Two days?"

"Yeah... He went back underground. They don't call him the mole for nothing! You know—"

"Yeah, yeah... Once he starts, he finishes."

"Yep. So, is it that serious?"

"More than you could know... I want to shut down an entire organization!"

***

On the drive home, the only thought going through my head is, How the fuck did Sienna find out?

I mean, as far as I know, she has no way of finding out about my other life. One thing I try to do is keep my face out of the clear. Always wearing disguises, never frequenting the same places, and using my tech man Tavis Teams.

"Hey! Death! Long time no hear!" Tavis said.

"Yeah, yeah. Peep this Tavis, I just got a call from my wife and it's safe to say, she knows all about my second job."

"Well, that should be next to impossible." States Tavis, but here's the thing about me and Tavis's relationship.

We're both freelance contractors. So we both have this understanding. At any time I could receive a contract on him and at any time he could learn about one on me, but except other hitmen or women. A square such as my wife, it would be impossible for them to find out who either of us was. So if she did, that means there's a leak somewhere and both of us need to be aware of it.

"Well Tavis, I just got a call, and from my understanding... Yeah, she definitely knows. But I'm pulling up into my yard about to face the music."

"Well... Call me when you find out how much damage is done."

"Fo sho," I said, locking the door of my Benz, walking up to my home. Opening the door, I prepare myself for something next to impossible to deal with. What greets me is way more shocking than what I came home expecting.

"Daddy!" Shouts Natasha, running down the hallway full blast. Looking past my daughter, I expect to see Sienna. My face turns pale as the moon, my heart rate speeding up, at the sight of Hunter standing in the hallway casually, with his hands in the pocket of an expensive suit.

"Neiros." He smiles, "Long time."

"So... You're telling me, fine ass Temera has gone all power crazy on you?" Akema said to Tivia as they pack up for the next flight to Columbia.

"Yes... He's even kidnapped my mother, holding her until I pop up."

"Damn! So what's the plan?"

"Honestly... Akema, I don't fucking know. If I said I want to kill my brother, I'd be lying. Plus, I really don't want to take over the coke business, but..."

"Siding with Temera would also be siding with a war."
"Absolutely, my brother has always wanted to take over the world. Literally."

"Well, all I can tell you is, I'm behind you 100%"
Tivia looks into the eyes of Akema, knowing with certainty that this woman is willing to go to hell with her. And something tells her, that is exactly where they are about to go, straight to hell.

***

"Where's Sienna?" I asked Hunter.
"Oh... She's asleep."

"Willingly."

"Not by a longshot. There aren't too many people that know I'm alive... So I try to keep that to a minimum." He said as if this conversation was just a continuation of one we've had yesterday, without him disappearing and all.

"Why?"

"Did I fake my death?' He said, standing with a picture on the wall of me and my family, "Really, I got bored with this life... You see Neiros, the way I see things is like this" He turns towards me with a blank stare, "over the centuries, man has spent too much energy trying to figure out the unseen... Not one man can prove the concept of reincarnation, but me... In this physical realm, I can be reborn as many times as I chose. You see I've come to the ultimate awakening. No man can tell you with absolute proof to make it a fact, as to what your last breath is taken..." He holds his finger up,

"But, due to intelligent design, it would be illogical to believe once you die it's over... So fuck trying to figure it out, yet if you apply most of man's doctrine to this physical world... All that shit is possible."

"So, let me get this shit right. You took me through all that shit, just because you got bored with the way your life was going?"

"No, just this one." He smiles, "My son, reality on Earth has many different faces. In the mind of a drug addict, the drug is helping him cope with the bullshit that is thrown his way, yet the drug is allowing more bullshit to come at him. So in reality the man is insane. To him, he has his reality under control. We trick ourselves to create an alternate reality than the one that truly exists. So in essence, due to us deceiving ourselves, reality is what we make it." He comes closer to me, placing one hand on my shoulder. "You see Neiros, I've got maybe five different forms of existence going on at this very moment. I chose to exist in each of them when I want."

"Now." I shrug his hand off and he smiles, "So why are you back?"

"Of all questions you could've asked... That is the most important, the answer... Chess."

"Chess? As in the game?" I respond perplexed.

"Yes." He nods.

"What?"

"I see I've been gone for too long." He shakes his head,

"You've lost sight of most of the things you've learned from me."

"No... I haven't. It's just you've evolved to some other shit."

"True, very true." He shrugs his shoulders, "But, you'll catch on later. So... No thank you." He points upstairs to where I sent Natasha.

"Yeah... Thank you." I said, keeping my eyes on Hunter. Maybe it's just me, but even though I know he's changed, the change he's undertaken has totally changed his nature. It's a must for a person on the path of enlightenment to evolve. It's just natural, but Hunter's change has given him a totally different ore. He just seems too sure of himself. It's not arrogant surely. It seems as if it's factual.

"Well, you're welcome. But your wife is about to awaken... So, so long."

"Hunter lis—" I said, looking from Sienna to an empty space. Damn! That's the shit I've been trying to achieve. Hunter is like a damn ninja!

"Neiros," Sienna said, sitting up holding her head. "When did you get in?"

"About a minute or two." I lied, "Natasha is home."

"She is?" Sienna exclaims, "Where is she?"

"In her room, but before you go see her... We need to get this out the way."

"Oh, yes." She said, with a totally different look coming into her eyes. "Neiros, as I'm sure you'll agree... You're not

95

ready to be with one woman and I'm a one-man type of woman. So it would be best if we just part ways."

"Yeah, I figured that much, but what about what you said on the phone?"

"Hmm..." She purrs, "Calling you by your hitman name, Death, you should've taken the ring off." She points to my hand, and I cringe. Just when you think you averted all aspects... A fucking ring!

Sienna gets up off the sofa with a look of definite knowledge on her face. The way she stood up, was showing me a side of her that, in all our years together, I've yet to see, and they say you never know someone just because you think you do.

"Yes, you heard correctly. Well Hubby, I've got some secrets too. I've done my share of crimes in your world, but not as
Sienna Simmons... You may have heard of me as... Life."

The realization of her words. Even though they were coming directly out of her mouth, did not quite puncture my thoughts correctly. I mean, I've heard of the name Life in my circle, but to find out Sienna was Life.

"What! Are you serious?!"

"As Death." She chuckles, "Pardon the expression."

"For how long?"

"Oh, about five years. But darling, that is the least of your worries. I've accepted a contract on you." She said, and as if those were the magic words, we both drew our firearms aiming at each other.

"Oh, ain't this shit cute," I said. "Some ole Mr. and Mrs. Smith shit."

"Not quite, we'll never work together." She said, pacing in a circle with me, trying to find cover.
"Natasha?"

"Of course I've thought that through, or you'd be dead." She said, with confidence, and truly, she's right. I came into this house not even thinking my wife was an assassin. "Here are the terms, I can't kill you; nor you, in her presence. Wouldn't want that kind of memory in our daughter's life."

"Why don't you just drop the contract?"
"Don't want to. Neiros, do you have any idea how many times I woke up at night and the only thing that stopped me from killing you is Natasha?"

"Why?"

"Answer this one question... Are you in love with me? If it was my life or yours, would you save me?"

"Si... I love you, but yeah, I'd be lying if I said I'm in love with you. If it came down to me or you," I shrug, "Ma, you out of there."

"I've always known that. For me, it's not the same. I would put my life on the line for you and you would choose death for me. Not anymore, the war starts." She said, tucking her pistol away, an odd gesture for me coming from her. "Oh, by the way, you can have Natasha for the weekend. Now that I'm single, I'm going partying," She said, walking away.

"Hey," I said, "One question, when we meet on neutral ground." I smile, "You still gone give a nigga some pussy right?" I said, getting a smile out of her. "I told you bae, I'm fucked up."

"Yeah, Yeah, on neutral grounds. Because as sad as it is, when it comes to you, I'm fucked up too." She said, walking out of the door and when the light hit her face, I swore I saw tears.

Chapter 8

The next day, I decided to get away from the city for a day or two. So, I decided to take Natasha to Wild Adventures in Valdosta, Georgia. Walking the theme park, the breeze was kind of cutting a little. So we opted to stay away from the rides where water was involved.

These are the precious moments in life, that each man should live for. Just looking at the smile on Natasha's face, the innocent in her actions, makes me strive just that much harder. Sitting at an eatery inside the theme part, she swings her little head from side to side, her plaits swinging wildly around. The only thought that comes to mind is the fact that at some point, the reality of this world is going to spoil all of the innocence sitting before me.

So I question myself, do I try and shield her from this world or expose her to it with the hopes she'll shun the way I and others live? One thing I've learned is a caged animal goes wild when it's let loose, but a wild animal can never truly be tamed,

"Daddy... Why didn't mommy come with us?"

"Mommy is busy."

"Too busy to come and have fun?"
"Yeah... But speaking of mommy, I have something to tell you. You and mommy are going to be living by yourselves."

"Why?"

"Because me and mommy aren't seeing eye to eye right now."

"Well, I know why!"

"Huh, what? Why then?"

"Well silly! Because y'all have two eyes apiece."

"So." I smile.

"You'll need to be trying to look each other in the eyes... Not looking eye to eye! Duh!"

"Ha! Ha!" I laughed; I couldn't help but laugh at my daughter's answer. One thing about children is everything is cut and dry. Maybe that's where we as adults go wrong. Trying to have a million answers to the most obvious questions. "Well... Maybe I'll try that."

"You should," she said, with authority. "Me, you, and mommy are a family!"

"We'll be a family apart."

"No we won't." She pouts, "It won't be the same!"

"Listen baby, don't cry... You trust me?"

"Yeah."

"Then believe me when I say, we'll be okay," I said hugging her, and for the first time in my life, I actually feel as if I'm lying to the only person I truly love. Because truth be told, as things sit, me or my wife will have to die in order for one of us to live.

"Mr. Simmons?" Said a medium-height white man.

"Who's asking?"

"Agent Thomas Deals." "Mmhmm," I said.

Fuck! Now the damn Feds! Man, one thing about the creator, he must have a real thrill for dramatics. Because whoever he commissioned to write my life is on some real bullshit!

"How can I help you?"

"Well, if you wouldn't mind coming with me for a short walk." He motions to Natasha.

"Actually, I would mind... I'm trying to chill with my little girl."

"Well sir, this is not going to take more than a few minutes."

"If you say so," I said, getting up, walking to another table out of earshot of Natasha.

"Do you know this man?" Agent Deals asked, pulling out a picture of Gut One getting into his car. The thing is though, the feds never ask a question they don't have the answer to. But if they had me, I would be in cuffs right now. So why are they exposing their hand?

"Yeah, why?" I answer.

"What are your dealings with this man?"

"Listen Agent Deals, get to the point!"

"If you insist. We have an informant that was able to get Mr. Washington on tape admitting to the fact that you are the front man for his operation."

Aw shit! Now, this is that bullshit I was talking about! Sometimes a muthafucka thinks it's okay to talk! It's never okay to talk! "If so," I said, keeping my cool, "Why aren't I in cuffs?"

"Oh! That's a simple answer, that should be evident Mr. Simmons. I'm trying to get paid... Why else?"

It's mid-afternoon when Tivia and Akema land in Columbia. Walking through the small town of Balira, Tivia walks through, allowing the smells of her home country to remind her of the simple things in life she misses.

Walking by a stand, she smiles as the man tries to persuade her and Akema to buy some of the many assortments of fruits, from bananas to avocadoes, all the way down to plains, that is a usual ingredient in many of the native recipes.

"You know, I could get used to this simple way of living," Akema said, licking the juice from a mango off of her fingers.

"Yeah" Tivia sighs. "It seems simple, but with this simplicity, comes with a lot of struggles. A lot of people you don't see are in the fields slaving to make a living. And the pay they receive sometimes isn't enough to feed their family for a substantial amount of time. Not to mention, those that work in the factories end up becoming addicted to the cocaine they spend all day producing, cutting, and bagging."

"Yeah, that's the downside, but sometimes the good outweighs it."

"And what would that be?" Tivia said, with an interesting expression on her face. One of the main reasons she doesn't want to go home is the simplicity.

"Well," Akema says, looking around her and seeing a totally different view of what's before her. "Here Tivia, it's the small things that make people happy. Back home, everybody is so stuck on materials, glamour, trying to be the best, that we tend to lose sight of the most important things such as family, you know. How many of us children have fond memories of something as simple as running through the hills of their homeland? The smell of the flowers as the Sun peaks over the horizon. Not many, compared to the ones that awake to the sound of gunfire. The smell of exhaust, and spend most of their day trying to learn the latest trend." She shakes her head at the thought. "So yeah, living here has its bad side, but for me... The simplicity outweighs the bad."

Tivia looks at her friends and for the first time sees something she's never seen before. As Akema looks at the children with a look of longing, the wind blowing through her hair, she realizes why this way of life appeals to Akema, because hers was stripped from her.

"So," Akema sighs, turning her attention back to Tivia,

"What's the next move?"

"Actually, I haven't the slightest idea...but, I'm open for suggestions."

"Well, for one, I think we had better get off the streets for a minute. Because honestly, we're sitting ducks at this moment."

"Yeah... Well, I've got to check on something first." Tivia said, turning around, walking into the chest of a 6'6" man.

"Okay... What you gotta check on?" Akema said, with her back turned. Turning around, she sees Tivia staring into the eyes of the man with complete fear on her face.
"Tivia." The man says.

"M... M... Marco. Where is Temero?"

Akema watches the exchange, trying to figure out the best solution. She can see that even though Tivia seems to be afraid of the caramel-skinned man, with hair long enough to seem feminine, she still notices that neither of them is making any hostile moves. Could Tivia's fear be an emotion only perceived in her mind?

"Temero." Marco smarts. "Halt, I wish I knew."

"You wish you knew?" Tivia asks, facial expression changing to curious.

"Well, since he's taken over, he's decided to start a new."

"Start a new?"

"Yes. He feels anybody that has any ties with his old life may be a problem later. Truly, the only reason I'm alive is because of you."

Tivia looks into Marco's face and sees the severity in his look.

"What do I have to do with you?"

As Akema watches the exchange between Tivia and Marco, she's blinded by the glare from some unknown object.

Shielding her eyes from the Sun, she scans the immediate area in search of anything out of place.

After an eastward search, she turns her head in time to see the glare that caught her attention. The scope on the top of a sniper's rifle.
"Tivia!" She yells, reaching out to her friend.

"Yea—" Tivia starts to reply but is stopped as a shot from the sniper's gun sends a dart into her neck.

Akema tries to come to her friend's rescue but falls short of her goal as the effects of a simpler dart's poison take effect.

"Well," Marco said, with a slight chuckle. "I guess that answers your question."

***

"You trying to get paid?" I said, looking at this crooked-ass officer. Now excuse me, federal agent.

I notice this dude looks like he's straight out of the military, with his low buzz cut, square jaw, and ocean blue eyes. Another thing that gives him away is how neat and pressed his suit is. Don't get me wrong, most federal agents are neat as well, but this muthafucka is over the top with his shit!

"Of course, Mr. Simmons. Yeah, I could've just turned over all of the information I've uncovered to my boss... Yet, the only thing that would've happened is, you'll go to jail and I'd still be making a measly eighty grand a year." He said, smiling with an air of certainty in his voice.

"Mmhmm... Well, how do I know you've got any evidence of me?"

"Oh! I see the whole informant thing isn't sitting in." He waves his hands in a circle. "Well, how about this... I'm pretty sure you know the name, Michelle Jackson? Oh, yeah! Well, we know" He points to his chest, "You get your cocaine from her." He said with a cocky smile that I wanted to smack off his face.
Fuck! Who is this nigga Gut One talking to! Michelle is the wife of Damone Jackson, drug lord of Duval, and head of the Dirty 9 Thieves. To my knowledge, nobody knows about me
and Michelle's arrangement but Gut one!

This is that bullshit! To be honest, the only person I can think of is this bitch Akema. Fuck all of that Hunter shit! But I have to get out of this shit first, "So, what are you asking?"

"Not much, not much at all. 50 grand and I keep my little secret from both of my bosses... Damone Jackson, and the Federal System."

"Hmm." I chuckle, getting the answer to my questions, "So you're playing both sides of the fence... How is that working out?"

"Whoa, whoa, whoa!" He waves his hand in front of him, with a joking smirk. "You're getting into a zone that is way over your head my friend." Agent Deals said.

"You think so?" I respond.

"Oh yeah... Listen, I understand you've got the whole record label and dope boy thing going on." He said, leaving me hanging as to how I'm getting in over my head, "My boss has made me a millionaire. Off you, I plan to become a triple-digit millionaire."

"Really! So why get paid off me and take the chance of Damone finding out?" I said, trying to draw him out.

"Two reasons," He dismissed my attempt. "One, I've got this side chick that has expensive taste, the money you give me will be mostly for her."

"Reason two?"
"Just plain ole greed." He shrugs his shoulders.

"Greed?"

"Yeah! It's the American way. And hey, what can I say? I'm a die-hard American. Beautiful ain't it?"

Sitting across from this greedy bastard, taking the entire conversation in and analyzing it, one thought pops into my mind.

"Either you're very sure of yourself, overly cocky, or just not too bright."

"Now, why would that be... Huh?"

"This is our first meeting. But you're telling me a lot of information about how you do things. Who you're affiliated with? I mean, I've got enough info to damage your life buddy." I said smiling, attempting some of his humor.

"Ho! Ho! Oh shit! You smart niggas! Oh man!" he said, wiping genuine tears of laughter away from his face. Immediately, he cuts his laughter short, exchanging it for a dead-on serious face. "Listen, you fresh out the hood, slightly educated, piece of shit! I could tell you about every skeleton in my closet since I was five and there isn't shit you can do about it! Take it for a bluff or for what it is, the fucking truth! This is what is going to happen. You're going to receive a text with banking info... If my demands aren't met, we'll see who's sure of themselves, overly cocky, or just not too bright." He uses his finger to emphasize his point. "So in the terms of you and the rest of your hood rats... Get that money up!" He said, returning to his smiling self, arranging his suit jacket as if something was out of order and standing to leave. The only thought that goes through my mind as he walks away, without even a glance over his shoulder was, it's definitely going to be a minute before I shake this muthafucka.

"Daddy," Natasha timidly says, coming over to where I'm sitting.

"Yeah, baby?"

"Are the bad men going to come back?"

"I hope not... Why?"

"Because they make you look sad... Are you going to be okay?" She asks, hugging me.

"Yeah, yeah," I said, making this possibly the second time I may have lied to my daughter.

***

"Fuck!" Tivia says to herself as she awakes to a splitting headache. She attempts to sit up but can't, as she finds herself shackled and chained from the chest down. Looking at the padding all around her, her heartbeat starts to increase. The realization that a bad situation just got worse settled into her mind.

"Tiviaaa! My dear sister." Temero says, coming into her view, as he comes to stand beside the coffin that houses his sister.

"You actually thought you'd be able to just come into my domain and do what exactly? Kill me?"

Tivia looks into the brown eyes of her brother, with enough rage to set the entire room ablaze.

"No answer huh." Mocks Temero. "Well, really, I don't give two fucks sister... At one point, I told myself I would try to reason with you. Attempt to persuade you to join me. Yet, in the end, I said to myself, why beat a dead horse? So, this is what I'm going to do." He claps his hands, "Just bury you alive! You, your friend, and our mother... If you make it out, you get to live."

"Temero! Leave our mother out of this!" Tivia pleads, trying to hold back the tears that threaten to break free. Knowing if she lets them go, the display of weakness would only fuel her brother's disdain for her.

"Honestly, sis," He rests his hands on the casket, with a sudden sadness in his eyes "I didn't want to have to kill either you or our mother...but," his expression hardens back to its original form. "Mother, mother threatened to take my life if I ever set her free. She spat in my face as well. I thought you both would understand the reason I had to do the things I did." He bows his head, his medium-length black hair hiding his face, "But I was wrong." He said, lifting his head, with fire in his eyes. "So... In a war, there will always be casualties. Do me a favor, die casually."

With these last, heartless words, Temero steps back, waving his hand, with the other in his pocket. Placing his hand in his other pocket, he watches as one of his men hooks straps to the coffin.

As the beeping sound from the crane starts, Tivia feels the casket leaving the ground. The tears she tried to contain, burst free of their barriers rolling down the side of her face. "Well, at least you're going to die in style. I spent a fortune on this box... Adios!" He slams the upper half of the coffin closed.

Tivia starts to hyperventilate, screaming words of compromise as the dirt hitting the top of her confined space, signifies the end is near. Saying a prayer in Spanish, she attempts to slow her breathing and prays for a miracle that as of the moment was not insight.

Chapter 9

As much as he hates to admit it, as he creeps in all black nearing his target. Hamzah loves the rush he gets from a mission. After strip-searching Diego's family, he found the residence of one of his cousins located in a boarded area outside of Jacksonville.

Walking in the woods about 100 feet from the house, Hamzah contemplates the fact that once this entire mission is completed, he'll finally be able to retire. To be honest, if not for his duty to Allah, he'd more than likely continue to be a hired killer, but unlike what the media and N.C.I.S. portray, all Muslims are not the radical, terroristic people they paint them to be.

Hamzah himself has met a lot of Muslims that have a false concept of what the word jihad means and how to act it out. Hamzah yearns to be the Muslim that Allah will readily admit into Jannah. He longs to become a Haji and get to experience the hajj as described by Count Eduardo Gioja, the Italian Muslim in a book he read named: Why Islam is our choice. In which the Count gave him a vivid description of being alone in the Arabian Desert, with miles upon miles of it stretching like the sea; Alone in the presence of Allah, like a grain of sand in his hands contemplating the stars. And absorbed in the imposing solitude, far from all the mysteries of this world and astonished by the infinity of creation. More and more persuaded that the more science discovers new prodigious and marvelous natural laws, the more we must recognize in them the endless power of Allah and what of the joy of consorting with his brothers-in-Islam—white, brown, or black— feeling no difference among them, and turning towards the Holy Ka'aba all together.

Hamzah pauses and lets his goals enlighten his soul, yet he knows for him to get to them, he has a mission to complete. So, in the woods, he makes a two-unit prayer on a piece of dry Earth. In the commencement of his last Rakat, he supplicates to his Lord to protect him and forgive him.

Standing up, he is not happy about what he is about to do but assured Allah will give him a way out of this life, be it with this last mission or death.

Back in his zone, he deploys all of the techniques the military taught him in special op's training. Pulling out his night-vision goggles, he continues to make his way towards his target.

Stopping to survey the area, he notices a two-man team hiding in the trees. This brings him up short, confusing him. From his intel, this cousin of Diego's is only a regular man, with no ties to Diego's drug trade. So why would he have lookouts in the trees? Moving closer, Hamzah turns on his hearing device.

"Man... Tom this surveillance shit sucks!" said one of the men.

"Yeah, yeah... The boss is really uptight about getting inside of this house. What's the big deal?"

"To my understanding, this Spanish dude is stealing money from his company."

"Okay, so why watch the house?"

"Well, from what I heard Pino and Vince talking about, the stupid fucker has a safe with a couple hundred thousand stashed inside."

"How are they so sure?"

"The boss is banging the man's wife."

"Whoa! You sure know a lot of shit!"

"Just nosey as—" Tom is cut short as a silenced shot is let go from Hamzah's pistol. Before the other man can react, he too falls victim to his 9mm. The two men fall from the tree, slamming into the ground with a mighty thud! Hamzah checks their pulse to confirm his kills. Satisfied with the outcome, he moves on towards the house with ninja-like silence.

One of the reasons he chose this particular family member, is this guy Miguel is married without kids. He refuses to kill kids. As for Miguel, he'll repent to Allah, due to his being disobedient, not for the actual fact that Miguel is dead.

"Oh Papi! Oh! Oh!" The passionate moans of a beautiful Spanish girl greet Hamzah's ears as he approaches a side window.

Looking inside he sees Miguel inside with two women, in the throes of a threesome. Realizing this is going to be a lot easier than he planned, Hamzah swiftly runs to another window, gaining entry to the house.

Walking down the hallway to the bedroom, the sounds of the ongoing sex capade gets louder. To the point, as he stands outside the door, it seems as if it's wide open.

Easing the door open, Hamzah enters the gun first, still not being noticed.

"Miguel!" His booming voice comes out demanding attention.

"Wh— What the fuck man!' Miguel said, pulling the Spanish girl on top of him as a shield. "Listen, listen, listen! If it's money you want, I've got plenty! Just name your price!" He smiles.
While Miguel speaks, Hamzah stays completely silent. He has no intention of taking the money for himself, for greed has been the downfall of many nations, and he is only a man.

"How old are you?" He asks the Spanish girl, seeing the innocence of her youth, in the childlike features of her face. Not to mention the ones that grace her body.

"Sev, sev, seventeen." She says, voice quivering.

"And you?' He said, monitoring with his pistol towards the African-American girl.

"Who? Me?" She answers. "Um, um, eighteen."

"Don't lie!" Hamzah states, the look his eyes giving the young girl, being enough to make her drop her head, whispering

115

"Sixteen."

Turning a fiery gaze on Miguel, Hamzah steps forward. "Hey, hey, hey!" Miguel starts. "Man, I'm just trying to give them a chance of survival... If not me, then somebody else, you know?" Miguel said, as a form of defense.

With an aggravated gesture, Hamzah said "Okay, okay, listen Miguel. This is what's about to happen. I know you've got a couple hundred thousand dollars in this house. I want it."

"No problem man! What's the cost of life, huh!" Miguel swiftly pushes the Spanish girl off of him, running to the safe in the wall.

After removing a large family portrait, he starts to enter the code, unlocking the safe. As soon as he presses the last digit, opening the door, both of the young girls let out a bloodcurdling scream. When Hamzah's pistol places Miguel's forehead along with most of his brain on the door of the safe. Opening the door the remainder of the way, Hamzah pulls the money out of the safe, placing it into two neat stacks.

"What're your names?" He asks, using a piece of blanket to wipe the money somewhat free of Miguel's blood.

"Con... Consuela." The Spanish girl stutters.

"Tiffany." Replies the black girl.

"Alright Consuela, Tiffany... My name is Hamzah. Now you know my name, but not my face. This is the deal, I'm going to give you this money, and you're never going to do anything like this again... Are you in school?"

"No." Both girls said, in unison.

"Then enroll, but here's the catch, I'm a very resourceful man. I'll be checking on both of you. If you do the opposite of our deal, you'll join Miguel here. So, we have a deal?" Both girls shook their heads yes. "Alright get out of here."

Hamzah watches as the young girls scramble to get their belongings together, knowing he'll more than likely never see them again, yet hoping his threat was enough to scare them straight.

"Sir," Consuela says.

"Ma'am," Answers Hamzah.

"Umm... He brought us here." She said, twisting her fingers.

"Well, use his car to get where you have to go. Then burn it."

"Yes sir... And thank you."

"Consuela, you'll only be thanking me if you keep your side of the deal."

"I will sir, I promise." She said, with one of the most beautiful smiles Hamzah had ever seen.

Hamzah turns in time to watch Tiffany as she starts to walk to the bedroom door. Just as he's about to turn back to

Consuela, Tiffany is thrown back into the room from the force of a .45 caliber slug slamming into her chest. Immediately going into action, Hamzah drives forward, taking Consuela with him across the bed for cover.

Before the two armed assailants can get completely down the hallway, Hamzah shoots out the only light in the room, sliding down his night goggles in one smooth motion.

He watches as the men search for the light switch. Moving as silently as a cat, he creeps up on the first man, sliding a finely sharpened knife across his throat, while covering his mouth. Figuring, even the smallest gurgles will alert the other man. He drops the man's body, immediately getting out the way the second hitman fires off three wild shots. Coming out of a roll, Hamzah pulls out his pistol, placing three well-placed shots into the man's body. Killing him instantly.

After walking down the hallway, putting on the light, he returns to find Consuela crying over the body of Tiffany. Knowing there wasn't much he can tell the young woman to ease the pain, he brings the sheet full of money, placing a hand on her shoulder.

"Does she have any other family?"

"No." She looks up at Hamzah with a loneliness that shatters his heart to pieces, "No, we were all we got."

"I know this is going to be hard, but we have to go." He pushes Consuela's frame away from Tiffany's body.

Once he was finally able to get outside, he commands her,

"Run! Run into the woods!" He points. "I'll take you to where you have to go."

Hamzah watches as she heads for the woods, then goes back inside the house, setting everything on fire.

Walking into the woods, he finds Consuela huddled at the base of a tree. The moment she looks up, they lock eyes. He knows there's no way he'll ever be able to leave her in this world alone.

***

As she lays in her tomb, the darkness is so dense, it feels as if it is crawling all over Tivia's skin. It's only been a couple of hours, yet in her mind, it feels like an eternity. Trying to use the least amount of energy possible, she stays still thinking about the possible fate of her mother.

She knows her brother well enough to know he wouldn't subject their mother to the same fate as her. Yet she also knows he's not above killing her either. She believes her mother's promise to kill Temera, just on the love for their father alone. And she can be pretty sure Temera does too. To think, when they were young, their mother would always tell their father that Temera was off a little bit. I guess her intuitions were correct.

Shedding tears for her mother, the silence starts to play tricks on her mind. For Tivia can swear on a stack of Bibles that she hears scratching sounds, yet in an attempt to not go insane before she dies, she shuts the sounds out with thoughts of Akema.

119

Part of her wants to blame herself for Akema's death, but the other side of her knows there wasn't any way possible she could've convinced her to allow her to come to Columbia alone. Yet, that isn't an excuse for underestimating Temero.

Suddenly, the scratching sounds became deafening. Tivia tries to convince herself it's just the lack of air in her brain, causing her to hallucinate. To confirm her thoughts, a bright light pierces the darkness, blinding her, forcing her to accept the truth. It's over. She's dead.

The pull of the light forces her to cry out, "No! No! I'm not ready! Please God! I'm not ready to die!"

Struggling with the last bit of energy she can master, she tries her best to stop the inevitable, but the force coming from the light is too strong. Tivia feels her body being raised, rather her soul. She knows her physical body is still however many feet underground.

Finally, she gives in to the light, knowing there's no point in resisting.

"Tivia! Tivia!" A voice sounding much like her father's calls out.

"Oh papa! I'm coming, papa!"

"Tivia, wake up!" A second feminine voice commands.

"I'm sorry mother, so sorry! I should've saved you." Tivia sobs.

"Tivia, you're not dead! Wake up!"

Tivia hears the words, yet they do not register, "It's okay, it's okay mother. I can accept it. You don't have to lie."

"This bitch is tripping!" Akema said, splashing a cup of water on Tivia's face.

"Huuult!" Tivia gasps, opening her eyes, sitting up, looking around frantically. Once everything comes into focus, she starts touching her face and body to see she's real. "Oh! I'm, I'm not dead!" She shouts, elated.

"Bitch! I told you that shit a minute ago!"

A smiling Akema stares down at her, with Marco standing by her side.

"Marco!" Tivia yells, starting to lunge at him, "You treacherous son of a bitch!"

"Woah! Whoa!" Akema grabs Tivia, "He saved us and convinced Temero to spare your mother."

"Saved us?" Tivia looks at Marco then Akema perplexed.

"Yeah... He paid the funeral parlor dude to rig the caskets with enough oxygen to last us a couple of hours... Till he could double back."

"Really?"

"Really." Akema nods her head, letting Tivia's shoulder go.

"But now Tivia," Marco interjects "You and your friend here must leave, soon."

121

"But... Mother?"

"Listen, I've had a talk with your mother and convinced her to play along until we can formulate a plan to take Temero down."

"You really think Temero is going to believe her and have a change of heart?"

"No," He drops his head, "Not the least, your brother is not the friend I've known him to be." He said with sadness in his words. "The only thing we can do is try to bid our time, and later kill the monster he has become."

"Okay." Tivia shakes her head, knowing Marco is right. The lure of power has turned her brother into a monster, and right now he has the upper hand, "Let's go home." She says to Akema then turns to Marco, "This may sound like a stupid question... But Marco, how can I really trust you?"

"The question," Marco responds, with a sincere look, "How can you not?"

Seeing that as of this moment, he's right. Tivia starts a slow walk towards the door, "You're right." She turns around, "But if not, I promise you, I'll get you. Even if it takes my last breath."

As Tivia walks away, Marco is convinced of her words, yet follows behind with his eyes on Akema. For the look in her eyes, says what Tivia's words conveyed, but a whole, not more.

Chapter 10

By the time they walked into his home, it was time for Hamzah to perform the Isha or night prayer. Feeling filthier than normal, he decided to perform ghuol, which is a purification bath, usually done after sexual intercourse. But tonight, Hamzah feels it's necessary after his day.

After he performs the bath, he stands under the hot water a little longer, allowing it to ease the tension out of his body. So absorbed in his thoughts, he jumps when the feel of hands on his back shatters his moment of bliss, throwing him into action. Spinning swiftly around, he grabs Consuela by the neck, forcefully pinning her against the back of the shower.

"What are you doing?" He exclaims through his gritted teeth. Totally surprised, Consuela clutches his strong hand around her neck, beating on his forearm until his grip eases and air can flow through her throat.

"Th, th, thank you." She meekly utters.

"Listen." Hamzah said, his eyes on the wall to avoid looking at her nakedness, "There's another bathroom on the first floor. Find it, shower, get dressed, and don't move from the living room sofa until I come in. Alright?" He releases her.

Consuela looks at Hamzah with an expression that he wouldn't ever think she would give. Then a quick thought emerges, and it's shocking to him that his actions would confuse her, for in her way of life, reality dictates that all men want the same thing, her body.

Swiftly following Hamzah's orders, Consuela finds the bathroom he spoke of, getting ready to shower. As she goes to turn the water on, her reflection in the mirror catches her attention. Looking back at her is a lightly tanned face, small nose, with small plush lips to match, but the look in her hazel eyes shows a history of the hardships she has endured.

At an innocent age of nine, Consuela was forced into a life of prostitution. Just when her mother's friend Semi found a group of men, willing to pay top dollar for young girls. Consuela was eavesdropping from her room and heard Semi telling her mother how the men paid her handsomely a year ago for her daughter Aisha.

Not thinking that she was in for the same treatment, Consuela decided to go back to bed. Plus the smell of crack cocaine they were smoking was giving her a headache.

It was until five days later, that she realized the conservation that she'd overheard, was a preview of a life of horror, being plotted for her.

Walking into her home, she paused, her heart dropping at the side of a living room full of unknown grown men, all undressing her, with eyes full of lust.

"Yeah... Evelyn." One of the men said as Consuela's mother spun her around modeling for them. "You've definitely got a nice looking youngin there, how old is she?" He said,licking his perverted lips.

"Nine."

"How much?"

"$1,500."

"A piece or together?"

"This is her first time, only one of you this time."
"Normally I'd say no... But I'm sorry boys, y'all gone have to catch the next ride." The fat white man said, to a room full of groans of disapproval from his friends.

Following her mother's orders, Consuela goes into the bedroom, only to run out screaming when the man pulls his pants down.

"Mommy! I'm scared!" She said, tremors running down her underdeveloped body.

"Connie." Her mother said, hugging her closely, "You have to do this for mommy, you have to do this for us okay? It may hurt at first, but the pain will go away—"

"It always does," Consuela says, finishing the words her mother told her the day her innocence was taken away. And now eight years later, for the first time in her life, Consuela meets a man that refuses to take the one payment all men she's ever met have never refused.

For the first time in her life, she looks at her reflection, questioning her beauty. Evelyn always told her that with her beauty, no man would be able to refuse her. Could she have possibly been wrong?

After her shower, she walks slowly into the living room to find Hamzah has beat her there, waiting patiently with a book in his hand. A closer inspection reveals he's holding

125

the Quran in his hands, a contemplating expression on his face. Looking up, he only smiles and says "Sit."

After a brief pause, he sits the Quran down with a gentle look on his face she never thought he was capable of possessing.

"Consuela, I have a feeling that you've led a life of destitution, shame, and other despicable words. But if you'll let me, I want to help you change that. First, I'm Muslim, just so you know.
So don't you ever in your life come around me naked again! I don't want your body. I don't want sex from you. I just want to help you."

"Why?"

"Solely for the sake of Allah... Therefore, it's one of my duties to him as a Muslim."

"Ain't Muslims like terrorists or something? Don't they beat their woman?"

"Not all... just the deviants. One who follows the guidance of Muhammad, rightly, wouldn't harm anyone without a just cause, but living with me, you'll learn more about Islam."

"You're going to make me a Muslim?!" She said, appalled.

"No! No!" Hamzah laughs at the expression on her face, "I can't force you to become Muslim. You'll learn, because you'll have questions, but back to the matter at hand. In that sheet is over one hundred thousand dollars, all of it is yours.

"Okay, and what do you want?"

"For you to succeed, you can live here until you feel you're able to move out on your own. You don't have to decide now.

I've got some business to handle. There's plenty of room for you to sleep and food to ea—"

"I'll stay."

"That easy huh?"

"Yes." Consuela shakes her head with a tear in her eye.

"Whoa! Why are you crying?" Hamzah sits down next to her.

"Because," She wipes the tear away, "My heart is telling me to believe you... But my mind is telling me in the long run, I'm

going to regret this decision."

Sienna sits in her luxurious living room inside of a $100,000 house she purchased years ago in the outskirts of Jacksonville, in an area called Meclony. Sitting on her sofa, she contemplates how she and Neiros got to the point they are at right now.

For her to say she doesn't love him, she would be lying to herself. It's his infidelity that has made her loath him. It seems as if day in and day out, he's cheating, and his answer of being addicted to women is just one more reason for her to rid his influence from their daughter's life. Yet that is always the thing that is on both sides of the fence, she is forced to ask herself if she is just trying to find justification for the fact she's just sore that Neiros broke her heart.

"Hello, Edward." She answers the phone with an all-business tone.

"Well, hello to you, too busy?"

"No, why?"
"Well, I know you've got the whole Death contract going... But you've also got another problem to solve."

"And that is?"

"Someone has put a hit on you."

"Mmhmm." She says, sitting up slowly.
"Yeah... And someone tells me Death is going to be the 1st person contacted to take the hit."

"Ed, what the fuck is going on?"

"Honestly honey, I've got the slightest fucking idea. But someone is paying damn good money to pit the best against the best. You and Death aren't the only ones... There are about three other sets of assassins that have been contracted to kill one another. The thing is, all of you lead such a private life that no one can make the connection. If not for you telling me that you and Death were married, I'd be in the dark as well."

Hearing the words out of Edward's mouth, Sienna thinks about putting her situation with Neiros on the back burner. It's one thing to want to kill him for her own personal reasons, but to satisfy someone else's sick game is a different situation in itself.

"Edward, let me call you later." She said as Neiros and Natasha walked into the house.

"No problem."

"So, how long have you had this?" Neiros said, looking around the house.

"Trust me, you'd prefer not to know."
"And why is that?"

"It'll make you question a lot of my actions since our marriage began."

"And... You don't think finding out your little secret didn't?"
"Once you really start analyzing things, you'll see it was never really a secret." Sienna said, "Tasha baby when you go upstairs, the second room on the left is yours, okay?"

"Yes ma'am," Natasha answered, hurrying to see her new room.

"Well, what's up?" Neiros said, with an all-too-familiar look on his face.

"Not that!" Sienna exclaims, "Damn is there ever a time you ain't thinking about sex!"

"Actually." He said, contemplating the question "Yeah." He answers, with that smile that always seems to melt her heart.

"But hold on." He said, checking a message on his iPhone.

"Damn... Ain't that some shit."

"What?"

"I've just been offered five million dollars to take a contract on you." He smiles.

"That..." sighs Sienna, "is exactly what I wanted to talk to you about... I was talking to my handler when you came in. He said multiple contracts have been put out, aiming to pit two assassins against each other. So, I'm putting my contract on you on hold."

"Yeah... So, what do you say? Temporary truce?"

"I'm all for that... but why can't the truce be permanent?"

"Honestly..." She says, eyes cast on the ground.

"I wouldn't have asked if I didn't want an honest answer."

"Well Neiros, I've been wanting to kill you for years now."

"Damn! Why is that?"

"Do you really have to ask that question?!" Snaps Sienna, pausing to get control of her emotions, "Since we took our vows, I've given you all of me. Can you stand here and tell me that you've ever done the same?... Exactly." She said, upon seeing the expression on his face, along with the silent response. "Exactly... The only one that mattered to you, is you!"

"Whoa! That's not true!"

"Please!" She cuts him off before he could defend himself.

"Your actions can tend to be an image of your true self. How many times have you left me and your daughter alone to be in the bed with some two-bit bitch?!"

"Don't bring Natasha into this! You know I love my daughter."

"You do, do you? Okay, tell me Neiros. Mr. I love my daughter; in a week how many times does your daughter watch a T.V. show? Huh? I'm waiting!" Sienna said, knowing the truth of his actions is hurting his heart from the expression on his face.
"Listen Si... You know damn well how demand—" Neiros is cut short, as Sienna slams a solid punch into his jaw. As the next one comes speeding his way, he swiftly sidesteps the too accurate strike.

"Whoa! Ease yo ass up!" He exclaims, putting a little distance between them.

"I'm going to ease up alright... Muthaufcka I'm damn sho gone ease up!" States Sienna, making a move to grab something to throw. "Got something for your Muthafuckin ass!"

Seeing that at this point he has two choices, Neiros goes with the ones that give him the best results.

Grabbing Sienna in a bear hug, he slams her on the sofa, smothering her mouth with a kiss. Only to let out a smothered scream, when a knee connects with his groin.

"Get your ass out of my house!" She yells, standing over him pointing at the door, as he nurses his injuries. After a minute or two, Neiros slowly gets to his feet, hobbling to the door. All the while being followed by a laughing Sienna.

Once he's outside, she stands in the doorway with a big grin on her face.

"Now that's how I like to see you... On your dick!" She says, slamming the door. Once the door closes, she leans against it, laughing, really wanting to cry. Because as much as she hates to admit it, the only man that can make her act like the hood she was raised in, not like the sophisticated woman she's grown to be is outside on her lawn in pain, but she still feels
that one day, she'll have to kill him or him her.

Chapter 11

Once I get in my car, I pause to think about what exactly just took place. Not only the whole game somebody is playing, because truthfully, you can't stress something you don't really know about. But my relation with Sienna and the state it's in now, yeah, I stress that, because mainly it may be my fault. To be honest, she made some valid points. But in my defense,
I actually do be working at night. I fuck hoes, pardon my French, during the day. Really, I've got to tighten up, just on the strength of Natasha.

"Gunsmoke, what's up?"

"Shit... What's up?"

"You still in the Ville?"

"Yeah, I'm going back to Coca tomorrow."

"Well, tonight you coming to the club with me."

"Shiit! On you, I'll be there."

"I ain't say all that shit!" I joke.

"You ain't have to... Which club?"

"The Globa, Murder doing a show with Killer Chris from the D9 shit."

"Murder?"

"Oh, I ain't tell you about the white boy I signed?"

"You signed a cracka!"

"Yeah."

"Oh shit homey! You really trying to go out of business."

"Brah, you trippin... This cracka raw!"

"Aight, if you say so. We'll see you tonight, but um... Damn bitch! Watch them teeth! My shit sensitive!"

"Brah! Who the fuck are you talking to?"

"Oh... I ran across this little bunny ya feel me. Got her eating a nigga up a little piece."

"Brah! You could've told me you was busy."

"Brah! You ain't ask. Ouch, bitch! I said watch them fucking teeth!"

"Brah, handle ya business."

"Yeah brah... Cause I'm about to choke this bitch, she scathed my shit again!"

"Tonight," Gunsmoke said, hanging up.

By the time I was done talking to Money, which by the way is a name most people call him, but I ain't most people. So I call him Gunsmoke, I start to turn on Pearl St., so I can have a little conversation with Gut One.

As much as I want to blame Akema, the mathematics just don't add up. I'm almost sure if she'd felt Gut One was a liability, she'd have pulled my coat to that shit. Call it a hunch, gut feeling, or maybe I'm tripping, but I just feel shawty solid.

Pulling up to a stop in front of another one of our trap houses, I approach Gut One as he stands over another male who is brown in complexion with his shirt off, showing off the many tattoos that cover his body.

When the man attempts to stand up, Gut One backpedals, allowing him to regain his footing.

"Come on! Come on fuck nigga! Get yo pussy ass up!"

"You got it, brah... You got it!" The man said, stumbling as he attempts to stand, "You won brah... I'm straight."

"Nigga you got me fucked up! You gone come to my shit, and front me about a bitch that ain't even yo ole lady! Just because you fucking her... Nigga you straight when I say you straight."

Seeing he had no way out of the situation but to fight, the man squares off, approaching Gut One. Throwing a sloppy combination, the man makes my little nigga look like Floyd Mayweather, the way he weaves and sidesteps his advances. I watch in a somewhat state of awe, as Gut One shoots two well-aimed jabs, weaving another sloppy hook, countering with a swift three-punch combination.

Thinking back to when I first met this nigga, his fight game has definitely improved for the better...

"Damn Tanisha!" I said at the age of sixteen. At this moment in time, I had pretty much solidified myself up as an upcoming boss in the streets.

Sitting on the back porch of my apartment in Heron Walk, well, one of my places of residence due to the fact that it's in the mind of my mother. I still lived with her and I could always go to my older chick Tammy's house out on the westside.
Y'all are most likely thinking how at the age of sixteen I have my apartment. It's quite simple actually. As I've stated, I've been hustling, doing little side jobs since thirteen. At sixteen, I'm to the point I can move about an ounce or maybe two every other day, and I had no bills. So I was just stacking money.

With that much income coming in, I got Hunter to get me a place in his name. So here I am talking to this little fine chocolate-skinned honey, trying to figure out how to get into her pants.

"Damn! What boy?" Tanisha said, trying to play hard to get.

"So that's how you gone play it?"

"Boy, I got a headache."

"I got some aspirin."

"Damn! That's the only reason you brought me way over here is to try and get in my stuff!"

136

"Nah." I lied, "But, I ain't gone lie and say it wasn't one of the reasons."

"What's the other one?" She said, with expectations in her eyes.

"You know a nigga fucked up about yo big-headed ass."
"Boy! My head ain't big!" Tanisha replied, patting her hair. But shit! She knows a nigga was telling the truth. When we go anywhere, I can just barely see shit out of my passenger side window.

One of the reasons I'm frustrated, she just won't let a nigga fuck. Yea, she did give a nigga some head, and every time she does, she always complains about her neck hurting afterwards. That's that big ass head! I told her ass she needs to work on her neck muscles. Shit, by the time she's thirty, she gone need a neck brace just to look a person in the eyes.

"Bae," I smile, "You know I love yo big ass head, so why you trippin?" I said, kissing her on the forehead. Because aside from her big ass head, she's Portuguese and Black. So she's got this long-ass pretty hair that stops at the beginning of her medium-sized ass. One of her best features is her smooth skin, but those green eyes are a muthafucka too!

"Whatever boy!" She said, rolling her eyes, and I can't help but focus on her neckline allowing my eyes to travel down to her size A breast. Looking further down, I can tell her stomach is flat as hell, but my mouth starts to salivate as I look at the little midget sitting between those thick ass thighs. I can't wait to put them shits on like a pair of earmuffs.

After another thirty minutes of talking, I finally get Tanisha to get with the program. The moment I'm about to step into the apartment, I see the scrawny ass Git come running around the corner, straight to my porch.

"Whoa! Hold up, where you going, Git!" I said, which sounded odd, being I was only sixteen myself.

"Man! Look brah, let me hide in yo house for a minute!" He said, looking around frantically.
"What? You running from the police?" I said, equally looking around.

"Naw, naw... I ain't trying to get beat up."

"Git, you wildin! You better stand up, you only prolonging the inevitable."
"John-John!" Says a voice from behind him.

"Aw damn!" He exclaims. "Listen" He turns around,

"I ain't on this shit! Chill!"

"What? She got a brother you're afraid of?" I asked, looking at the little girl Gut One was talking to.

"Brother? I don't need no brother!" She exclaimed, hands on her scrawny little hips, head about to pop off her neck. "I did beat John-John up once and I'll do it again... He ain't nobody!"

"Come the fuck on!" I said, shocked when the little girl rushed Gut one's ass, beating him like Tyson did Spinks. No, I mean literally. The next thing I know, it was over and Git was asleep. To this day, when I joke about that shit, he always claims he didn't want to fight shawty, but I saw the fear in his eyes.

Since then though, little John-John became a straight beast, because as I watch the dude walk away, looking like he just went twelve rounds, I can honestly say the dude could fight, but Gut One was the better fighter.

Later on, after he got straight, it was time to get down to business. "Brah," I said, looking at my soulja in the eyes. "The feds come and holla'd at me."

"Really?" He said, and right at that exact moment, I knew something was wrong. The thing with Gut One is I raised this nigga. I know him like the back of my hand. When he answered my question and broke eye contact, I knew things weren't right.

"Gut... What ain't you telling me?" I replied, in a very serious tone, while scooting forward on the couch.

"What ain't I telling you?" He puffs his cigarette, eyes cast to the ground. "Honestly bro, the real question should be: What haven't I been telling you? So let's start from the beginning." He says, taking a deep breath, yet he doesn't start talking. Instead, he puts the cigarette out, splits two Garcia Vegas's, rolling both of them.

After handing one to me, he settles back on his loveseat and sighs, "About a year ago I met this cracka named Steve while partying out in Ponte Vedra with this bunny. He started telling me he was a businessman and after a couple of minutes, he started talking about drugs and shit. So, long story short, I started popping buddy off about two bricks every other month. So about a week ago, this other white dude comes...and this muthafucka is the feds."

"Damn." I sighed. Because the thing is, I may have to kill my nigga. Why? Because a dead man can't testify. "Gut One," I continue in a neutral tone as possible, "Tell me you ain't through me to the wolves."

"Actually bro," He finally looks me in the eyes, "There was no need. When this crack showed up, he had pictures of me, you, and Michelle. So, I just gave him what he asked for."

"And that was?"

"Hush money."

"Hush money?" I allow the words to linger in the air.

"Yeah, round bout fifty stacks." Gut Once said, pulling on the weed-filled cigar, forcing the tip to glow like red hot as my temper was at the moment. Sitting back on the couch, I think of the only possible solution to this situation...

"Jizzle, what's up?" Michelle's lovely voice says over the waves.

"Problems."

"As in?" Michelle questions, but here's the low on her, Michelle is really about the life she's living. I mean this chick got police bodies in the graveyard. Now, don't think she's the type to overreact. Not in the least, but she ain't got no problem flipping our little federal friend.

"You know a slimy ass cracka named Agent Deal?"

"Yeah, Ben... Ben Deal. He's on Damone's payroll. What's up?"

"Well, the mutha fucka is extorting me. Says I got to pay him, or he'll tell Smoke about me and you and turn me over to the feds."

"Uh huh." She said, and for about twenty seconds, she's so silent. I almost thought she hung up, "First, you don't worry about Damone. The only person he's going to be mad at is me. As for Ben, let me see what I can do."

"That's what I will do."

"No problem, you gone be at the Globe tonight?"

"Yeah, got this artist on my team. He's performing with K.C. So yeah."

"We'll talk then."

"Alright... One." I said and hung up the phone.
Looking over at Gut One, he's got this odd expression on his face. "Gut One... God." I said, easing off the sofa.

As I come closer, I notice his eyes. They have the look of those on plenty of faces I've seen. That stare can only come from death.

Listen, I don't know if you've ever killed somebody before or seen a dead body. But for me, I see why they try and close their eyes. The only reason I say try is when you die and rig

141

Mortis sets in, the only thing a person can do is cover their eyes because the eyelids won't close. And that stare, it seems as if a dead man can see the thing that you'll cry over. As if he's looking straight through you, or doing what Gut One's eyes are doing now...accusing you.

"Damn," I said, thinking back again, to the day I stopped the slaughter taking place between John-John and the little girl.

Afterwards, I brought him to my apartment and got Tanisha to clean him up. Then we sat in the living room talking, "How you just gone let shawty beat you up like that?"

"Man." He puts his head down, "I ain't want to hurt her."

"Yeah." I laugh. "We'll let that be the reason!"

"For real man! She's just a girl!" John-John said, pushing up a little bit, not getting off the sofa.

"Whatever." I wave him off. "How old you is Git?"

"Twelve."

"Where you live at?"

"Around the corner with my mom." He said, and it's sad to admit, only then did I take notice of his appearance.

Git had some skinny ass legs that were exposed by his cut of jeans. I felt bad once I noticed how dirty he was and how nappy his hair was.
After a quick investigation, I found out his mom was on dope and he was just barely maintaining. So I put him on.

Now, looking in those dead eyes. The only question they seem to ask is: Why? Why did you bring me into this life? As I look behind my soulja, seeing the hole in the window that comes from the bullet that took his life, the only answer I can give is: My intentions were good, but the road to hell is paved with good intentions. In the end, though, I'm going to find out who did this. Granted, in my head, I feel I already know who's behind this. The reason being, because one loose link can allow the whole fence to become unraveled... That is a lesson Hunter taught me.

Chapter 12

It's happening dog, we bout to come up from the fact/ And just start jocking y'all, slapping y'all, snapping dog/ Don't even start to ask the happens dog/ We creepin through the fog/ Niggas is finna bash ya dog— Spits Killer Chris, later that night in the spacious night club called The Globa, located on Beach Blvd.

With as much space as the club has to spare, I am amazed that it's still packed to almost capacity, with a mob of loyal fans. Who's come out dressed in their best to support their local rap stars.

I sat in the V.I.P. section located right behind the dance floor, contemplating my life as it stands. The truth is, a real man will admit he has feelings, but it's how he allows them to control him that makes the difference.

Me personally, I'm not into emotions too much, so it's really hard to give a fuck, but I've got too much going on to say fuck it.
Take this situation with Sienna. Now, truth be told, I really just miss the pussy, yet to say I want to have to off my baby momma, would be going a little bit too far. Granted, I will if need be. So, I'm glad she's decided to call a truce until we figure out what's actually going on, and the fact she decided to send the baby upstate helped ease my nerves a bit.

Now as for this Hunter shit, honestly, this muthafucka is getting on my damn nerves. This whole popping-up shit, Hunter does nothing just for shits and giggles. So why at this point in my life would he pop up?

I also found out he did kill Gut One. How?
The muthafucka left me a text message. His reason, Gut One was a liability. The sad part is, in most ways, he's right, yet still, why now?

Also, did Akema know he was alive when she finally decided to pop up and if so, what is her part in all this madness? At least one of my situations is about to be clarified, I think as Michelle and Damone come walking into the V.I.P., making a path straight to me.

"What's the business?" I say, standing up as they get to my table.

"You." Answers Damone, with a natural look in his eyes that makes most of the hood fables believable. His eyes have a hardness to them that only years of hard times can give them.

As he stands in front of me, I can't help but notice the serious demeanor his body language gives off. From his long dreads that hang neatly down the middle of his back, to the way he stands with his hands nonchalantly in his pockets, shoulders squared, legs just the perfect amount of space between them. His entire demeanor state's he's all about business.

"Before we go any further, I ain't mad at you for doing business with my wife. But I do find it kind of fucked up you didn't find a way to come to me... Wait." He said, putting his hand up, still making eye contact with me. "I don't want to hear the whys or the excuses. That's only appropriate to kill anger, and as I said, I'm not mad. So, from this point on, you'll be doing business with me. And the league just got major.

How many businesses do you have?" He asked, referring to my trap house.

"I've got enough business space to maintain," I answered, not putting him too far into my game room. Don't get me wrong, this nigga is strapped, but he's got some real killers on his team. And they'll have no problem wiping me off the face of the Earth just for the fun of it.

You may be thinking that me being a hitman, that shit should not matter. That's where you have it twisted. A hitman's job is based purely on the element of surprise. All that bullshit you see in the movies, about the hitman just walking in and killing a dozen people to get to his target. Bullshit!

"That is a good answer." He smiles, "So how much stock can I invest into your company?"

"Mmm... What can you stand?"

"Mmm... How about one hundred shares?"

Damn! This nigga talking about one hundred bricks! At the current moment, I'm copying about ten every two weeks! How the fuck! Damn! What the fuck have I gotten myself into?

"Um... Um." I stutter.

"Listen, don't worry. I franchise." He said, smiling, sitting down at the same time.

"You franchise?"

"Absolutely, you see one of the keys to longevity in this game is franchising. Most niggas want two to three businesses that have ten to twenty shares invested in them. No. The key, ten companies share a piece. You allow me to invest one hundred shares. I'll franchise you out of fine stores, no extra cost to you" This shit is too good to be true. My power base will amplify tremendously with this arrangement, but one question "Why?" I ask.

"Why?" He shrugs. "Simple, Michelle is an anti-social social person."

"Anti-social... Social person?"

"Yeah. She doesn't do the whole friend thing, but she'll be friendly as fuck if she finds something about you she likes. So, I trust her judgement." With that remark, he waives the waitress over, who immediately beckons to his call.

"Hey Smoke." She said, turning to Michelle. "And how are you doing Michelle?" She says, with what I swear is pure seduction in her eyes.

Now don't get me wrong, Michelle is fine as fuck, but I don't think she's into girls. Also, I don't really know her like that either.

"What's up Tiny?" She responds. "You know we'll have our usual."

"Okay, and later on tonight as well." Tiny replies, moving in between Michelle's legs, which blows the shit out of me but changes not one inch of skin on Smoke's face.

"Damone, you fill up to it?" Michelle looks at him, putting emphasis on the word up.

"Well, Jizzle" He looks over at me. "You feel like having an after-party, after the after party?"

"It's whatever," I said, but damn! I know this nigga ain't got it like that! To be able to fuck your wife and another bitch! Shiiiit! I'd really settle down with that arrangement!

"Alright... Tinny, bring about three more friends to my suite at the Hilton downtown. Promise them ten grand for the night.
You know what it is."

"No problem." She says, laying down, kissing Michelle with so much passion. One would swear they've been together for at least a year or two, and from what I'm seeing and hearing. It may be possible.

Once Tiny leaves and returns with some drinks, Damone takes a deep swallow of his double Hennessey, looking over at me.

"So... I've heard you've got a problem with Ben."

"Yeah," I answer, finishing my drink, signaling Tiny for another round.

"Well, peep this... I want you to continue paying him and never mention anything about us meeting."

"O... Kay, but why?"

148

"One thing about Ben is he tends to over throw his ass every once in a while. In his mind, he's got everything under control, yet let's just say, because you can live on illusion doesn't make fiction a fact. For Ben, fiction is his reality."

Now, this nigga just put my whole situation in a statement. This whole time I've been living on illusion, yet as far as everybody was concerned, it's facts, but really the facts are just now coming to life.

"But won't he see me and you together conducting business?"

"How is that?"
"The man does surveillance on me. He had pictures of me and Michelle, along with other ones." I respond, but the look on Damone's face says it all. He has one of them smug smirks on his face that says, really?

"Yes," I said, looking over at Michelle. "You have surveillance on me."

"Actually," He starts, taking another pull on his drink. Then I notice something. This nigga doesn't have one tap of jewelry on. As for the way he's dressed, you can tell he more than likely spent only two grand on his outfit. Setting his drink down, he continues. "To be truthful, I was keeping an eye on Michelle... You've got to keep in mind, she's definitely a loose cannon. Not sex-wise, but she'll flip a bitch quick. And don't take this personal." He said, pausing as Tiny walked over with five females behind her. "Give me a minute Tiny."

"Alright." She answers, walking over about ten feet.

"But" Damone continues. "Despite your success, smarts, and status in the eyes of others... In my world, you're about significant as the sixty grand I'm about to blow on some pussy for the night. Pocket change."

In most situations, I'd be insulted and would've most likely fired on this nigga. But first, this nigga is saying this shit with a smile on his face. Secondly, it ain't like what he is saying isn't true. Let me give you a little background on Damone Jackson. From what the streets say, he was given the game by this old head named AC. He started with shit and murdered and robbed his way to the top. Starting fucking with the Zoe named Red Eyes and now he's pushing everything from weed to heroin. Not to mention he's got the D9T family into legal shit now. I mean this nigga has got to be the truth if some
Muslim nigga named Atif wrote a book named Anathema, all about this nigga's life. So, yeah, I can take what he's saying as the truth. But, that's neither here nor there.

"Yo Tiny!" Smoke calls tonight's entertainment over. And my nigga, entertainment it is! Tiny walks over with an assortment of flowers, a Spanish chick, Chinese, and some other exotic beauties.

"So," Tiny states with a broad sweep of the hand. "Will this do?"

"Jizzle?" Damone said, looking at me, and y'all know I'm addicted to pussy.

"So," I say, "Brah, fuck the after party! Let's hit the party after the after party now!"

"You know what?" Damone leans back laughing, "You and me gone get along just fine!"

At the same moment in time, Diego sits in his home watching the bank of video screens he's installed to amp up his security. In his mind, he's thinking maybe underestimating his opponent was a mistake, being that Neiros Simmons is becoming more of a thorn in his side more than anything, but something tells him he's more than likely to be the next target in line.

He must admit that sitting in front of all these screens for the past four days is definitely taking its toll, but he has to be next. Because as of the past week, the only family he has left standing lives outside the United States.

An hour later, his lids are heavy, eyes about to close, where his premonitions come true. He sits up, totally awake, as he sees two figures moving in all black with ninja-like stealth over the eastside fence of his property.

"Alberto!" He calls, his new head of security.

"I'm already on it." Returns Alberto to Diego over the walkie-talkies.

Diego watches in anticipation as his new team of killers box the two intruders into an impossible situation to escape. The sound of gunfire is deafening as the team lets round after round loose onto the duo. Diego watches with glee as the two bodies jerk uncontrollably, looking like the body of a cow that made the mistake of walking into a river full of flesh-eating piranha.

After what seemed like forever, the assault of bullets stops, the duo lying motionless on the ground.

"Alberto! Make sure they are finished and sever their heads for shipping!"

"No problem sir." Alberto answers and Diego watches as the teams form a tight circle around the two, Alberto walking in the center, unsheathing the machete on his side, grabbing one of the men by the head. He cocks the long blade back. Diego's eyes almost pop out of his head when the force from an unseen bomb sends Alberto, along with Diego's entire security team flying in different directions.

"What the?" Diego shouts as the video screen shows a lone gunman walking up and spraying his security detail with a blanket of .762's, throwing the assault rifle down, only to grab the other one slung around his neck, finishing the team off.
Diego's eyes search each screen frantically when a voice from behind him scares the rest of his courage out of him.

"Now, that was too damn easy!" says Neo, holding a detonator in his left hand, pistol in his right.

"Where did you! How did you!" Stammers Diego, marveling at how it could have been possible for this man to get past the
mass of videos he's kept all his attention on.

"Well," Neo said, as calm as a lake on a windless night. "You my friend, were so busy worrying about the main event, you couldn't possibly force yourself to believe it wasn't the main event...but, none of that matters now. It's over buddy... but hey..." Neo smiles, "most of the time I torture my victims. You, my friend, are lucky. I've got more pressing business to hand—"

Neo is cut off as the force from a .45 automatic sends a slog into Diego's head and he falls sideways on the floor.

"God damnit Kane! You just had to come in all gang ho and shit!"

"Hey bro!" Kane shrugs his shoulders. "You the one who said you had shit to do, and I've been listening to you gab and gab for too damn long," Kane said, waving the pistol around,

"So... let's go!"

"Alright, alright muthafucka, but... Question?"

"Take off."

"Who were the two idiots you got to come over the gate first?" "Oh... Them." Kane said, with a wicked grin. "Two cat burglars. I told them nobody was home and the place was loaded... Shit!" He laughs. "The dumb bastards were about to come in bare-faced until I told them to wear the mask for the cameras."

"How'd you get them to wear the explosives."

"Now that was classic." He smiles, "Told them the vest was bulletproof so if cops got behind them, they'd be straight in a shot out!"

"Boy... They weren't lying when they said drugs can kill." Neo laughs.

"Yeah, and in this case... Quickly!"

Chapter 13

It's damn near three a.m. as I and Damone stand on the balcony of his suite at the Hilton. Looking out over the city, this is one of the moments when taking the city into the palm of your hands seems as easy as putting a picture into your pocket.

The city looks defenseless looking at it from an aerial view. All the lights, trees, cars full of people, who're just driving around without any knowledge of your intentions, but we all know it's just not that simple. One thing about any city, it has a defense and it's the love all other hustlers have for the pursuit of money.

Yeah, one man can be on top for a little while, but nothing lasts forever, and history tells us that. Name one empire or dynasty that has lasted forever. Muthafuckas like Napoleon, Hitler, to simple shit as No Limit, have all had their time on the top, but just in the case of Napoleon. Haters on the inside caused his downfall. As for muthafucka like No Limit, whose sound just got boring, nobody would stay on top forever.

"Smoke," I said, sipping my drink.

"Yeah?" He answers, as we've both been fucking all night. I was glad when his homeboy Flow, some Dominican cat from New York, came and took some of the pressure off a nigga.
Shit, the only bitch that was off-limits was Michelle of course.

"What's going to be your move when it's time to give the top position to somebody else?"

"Now that's a good question." He said, passing a blunt my way. "But for me, that moment will never come."

"How do you figure?"

"Simple... I've never been on top." He replies, leaning against that banister. "Yeah, in your eyes I'm on top. But truthfully, I ain't. You see the outside and it's the inside of the clock that matters. All the little pins, cogs, and wheels and shit." I listen intently, because so far what he's saying isn't making any damn sense until he continues. "I could give myself that status, but that would be denying the fact I gotta cop from somebody else. I ain't doing this shit by myself... And it takes an army to take over a small village, and I'm one drug dealer in a large city. Tell me Jizzle, what am I on top of? Nothing. I'm just one man in a web of business, attempting to feed my family... So, for me, there will be no next move. No handing over the reigns, none of that shit. It'll just end when it does, however it does... And the ones on top, with the fields of coke and shit, will just find another spider in the web."

"You know what? In that light, that makes perfect sen—" I'm about to say, but I'm cut off by the sound of Michelle cussing somebody out.

When I and Damone rush into the room, we find her standing in front of Flow yelling, "You just had to shoot the bitch!"

"Listen!" Flow says, and looking at the dude. Him shooting somebody is the last thing you expect him to do. I mean, the dude's a straight pretty boy! I'm talking log hair, nice physique type of nigga. "Michelle, at least I ain't kill the bitch!"

"Flow! You shot the girl in both of her hands!" Says Michelle, with a dead serious look on her face.

"Well, she shouldn't have been trying to steal my shit... One thing I know, Smoke done paid the bitch good. So she's just being greedy." He states, with his hands up in front of him, in order to stop Michelle from hitting him.

"Hold on" Interrupts Damone, "We ain't hear no damn shots."

"I know." Flow smiles, waving his silenced .9mm.

"So... What are we going to do about her?" Michelle directs at Flow.

"Honestly," He shrugs. "I don't give a fuck... You can merc the bitch for all I care." Says Flow, looking over at the girl, who has her hands wrapped up.

"Damn! You had to shoot her in both hands?" Questions Smoke, and the crazy shit is, he looks as if he wants to laugh his ass off, with the smirk starting to turn into a smile.

"Hell yeah! Bet she won't steal from nobody else! Will you bitch?" Flow said, shattering Damone's resolve, as he burst into a fit of laughter.

"This shit ain't funny!" Exclaims Michelle, stomping her feet.

"Shiiiit!" Barks Damone, "Look at shawty!" He points, causing everybody's attention to aim towards the girl, sitting on the sofa, hands wrapped in towels, shooting daggers at Flow, as he joins Damone laughing.

"Flow! This shit ain't funny!" Yells Michelle.

"Look!" Flow evades Michelle's fist, "Blame that nigga Smoke! I was not going to laugh until he did! I swear!"

As crazy as this may sound, these muthafuckas are making a festival out of this shit. I watch and can't help but laugh too, as Michelle chases Damone and Flow around the room trying to hit them.

The entire time, the poor girl is just sitting on the sofa bleeding. Which is crazy, because she's laughing too!

About two minutes later, Flow stops in front of the girl, putting one of the pretty boys 'I'm the shit' faces on. Now in my mind I think, I know this muthafucka ain't about to try and talk to this bitch, yet with a look as serious as a lover boy trying to sweet talk his next victim. He looks at the girl, and squeezes both of her hands, getting a "Flow! What the fuck!" out of Michelle.

Flow pulls the girl completely off the sofa, as Michelle tackles him to the floor, screaming at him. As he balls up to protect himself from the barrage of blows she runs down his body. Michelle came to a stop when the girl taps on her shoulder. Looking over her shoulder, Michelle's body goes limp when the girl says "Gotcha!", holding up both her hands, towel free, perfectly fine.

"Uhh... Uhh," Michelle states, looking back from Flow to the girl. "You muthafuckas! Oooh, I'm a get yo ass!"". She shouts, scrambling to get up and chase the girl. The tension in the room immediately eases down, yet as they run around the room, I notice I've seen this girl from somewhere before...

...2 years earlier...

"So wat's up with you tonight shawty?" my homebody Taylor said. He had just come in from Cali to visit me on some business-type shit. Sitting on the head of the Benz he rented for the week, he's talking to this fine ass redbone, with a short Halle Berry cut. Me, I'm sitting in the car smoking, behind the tent.
As my nigga spits some of that west coast game at shawty, I try to get a good look at her, but the glare from the moon is bouncing off the windshield, causing the light to block most of her face. Then she moves, and damn I must admit, shawty is cute as fuck.

"Yo Jizzle!" Taylor said, opening the car door.

"What's up brah?"

"Shit, I'm about to see what's poppin with this little bird I met... What you got planned? She said she got a friend."

"Well, Shit! You know I'm bout that!"

"Alright," Taylor said, about to spin around, when the barrel of an A.K. 47 was placed on the center mass in his chest.

The fucked-up part is, I should've seen this shit coming. But as of late in that year, I had started relaxing in my businessman mode a little bit too much.

"You niggas got a real nigga fucked up!" Taylor said, looking at the man with anger in his eyes.

In a situation like this, your options are severely limited. The thing is, I don't know exactly how many muthafuckas are outside. Yet the facts are: One nigga got the jump on Taylor, and what he's carrying has enough bullets to kill both me and my nigga.

So, being the nigga I am in a jam, I look to Taylor to see what his next move is. Because the truth of the matter is I can make out of this shit alive, but depending on what Taylor does, his chances can either be high or slim to none.

"Nigga, fuck—" was all Taylor got out of his mouth before the assault rifle opened up, sending multiple rounds through his and my body. I watch calmy, knowing to panic would be the end of my life, as Taylor's body slams into the car, falling slowly to the ground.

I decided to play dead or at least unconscious, knowing that most jackboys are like bears... An inanimate body that poses no threat.

Slowing my breath down, by tuning out everything that doesn't matter, my body appeared to not even move an inch, as the jackboy came around to my side of the Benz to inspect me.

"Nate! Jo-Jo! Check the trunk and shit while I take care of the inside!" He said, and then came the hardest part of all. It took all the strength in my body to keep the façade up when he pulled me out of the car, throwing me to the ground like I was a piece of trash.

"Yo! Tee!" shouts Nate. "Boy! This nigga loaded1" He exclaimed, holding up the three bricks of cocaine Taylor had just purchased from me.

"That's what the fuck I'm talking about!" whoops Tee, "God damn! You did your thang—"

***

"Quiesha," I said in the present time, receiving a shocking look out of the girl in front of Flow.

"Who's Quiesha?" Smoke asks, looking at me.

"Smoke," I said. "What that bitch on the sofa say her name was?"

"Monica... Why?"
"Boy, that is my name," Quiesha says, standing up, but stops in mid-motion as a gun appears in Flow's hand like he's a magician, and he points it two feet from her breast.

"Whoa, whoa, whoa little momma... Why you cutting son off? Yo son, what's the deal with this bitch?" He says.

Damn! I might have underestimated this pretty boy ass chico. Most muthafuckas wouldn't have caught how ma was trying to evade the situation by causing confusion, at the

161

same time putting distance between herself and the nearest threat.

"This is the deal." I start, the pleading expression on Quiesha's face almost, for a split second, making me want to switch up, but the bitch might be plotting. So it's best not to take any risks. "This bitch set my nigga up to get robbed, and the fuck niggas she was with merced my nigga Taylor."

"Now! You ain't talking about Taylor from Cali?" Flow said, a shocked expression on his face.

"What? You know that nigga?" I respond, equally shocked.

"Red nigga, about yay high." He indicates by putting his hands under his eyes. "From Long Beach, but moved to Rancho Cucamonga... Yeah, used to come up to sell a nigga some high-grade shit. Damn, this bitch set bra up! You fucked some good money up hoe!" He said, then with the speed of a cobra hit Quiesha with the barrel of his pistol. "So, what you wanna do with the bitch?" He asks, standing over her, pistol inches from her face.

I look down at Quiesha, laying down on the plush carpet with blood leaking out the side of her face. And honestly, I can't feel one bit of remorse for the bitch. Truth is, she brought this entire situation upon herself. So, trying to look all pitiful in the hopes that her smooth red skin and wavy hair, will make one of us lock into them honey-brow eyes and forget what she did and just smash that ass from behind. Y'all know what? I got some real issues. Here I am thinking about sex in the middle... Yeah, I'm fucked up!

"Room service," comes a feminine voice, cutting off my sexual thoughts and my chance at answering Flow's question.

"Let me get it," I said, pulling my pistol out, taking the safety off.

One thing that has always pissed me off about movies is this. A real killer keeps his gun cocked and ready. Not because he's paranoid or because he likes killing people, but for reasons like this. As tell-tale this as this is, it's common sense what's about to happen next. We caught the bitch up, so it's time for her rescuers to get the room service bitch to get us to open the door. Just as I have explained it, it's evident from the expression on the woman's face when I look out of the peephole. So, if I had to cock my pistol, they would've known we are on to them.

The woman's frantic glances left and right tells me there is more than one person outside the door with her.

Signaling to Flow, Damone, and Michelle, we all gather around the door.

"Hold on a minute ma'am... I'm trying to get dressed. This must be the champagne I ordered, right?"

"Yes sir." The woman said, in a thick Spanish accent.

Once everybody is set, I put my hand on the doorknob, pulling it open, at the same time I hear the lock on the adjoining suite click at the same time, but also at that moment I realize we've been had.

163

Everything slows down as I spin around remembering one vital fact: This is the Hilton. Suites don't connect. "Fuck." yells Flow, opening fire as three men enter in all-black come out of the bedroom into the living room with the women in front of them.

One of the shots Flow sent hits Tiny in the stomach sending her to the floor, but the sound of an assault rifle cocking and that Spanish accent saying "Don't fucking move!" causes all of us to stop, putting our hands up.

"Mm, mm, woo!" laughs Smoke.

"What's so damn funny?" Tee said, coming across the living room attempting to intimidate Smoke. But if he'd done his homework, he'd have known this is the last man in Duval that is going to be crying in the face of death.

Smoke looked Tee square in the eyes, smile still plastered on his face, casually placing his hands in his pockets. "You are, you are what's so funny."

"Really? And how's that?" Tee said, with a cocky grin.

"Um... Do you know who I am?"

"Yeah, I do."

"No you don't... You can't and this is why." Smoke said, holding up a keychain on which a button has been pressed.

"Prevention is my Mastercard. Never leave home without it."

The smug look on Tee's face dissolves the moment he discovers that the only people in the room, that don't have red beams on them, didn't come with him. The fake room service lady gulps loud enough for the entire room to hear, causing me to turn to see what is the reason their cockiness has disappeared.

Standing across the hall with the door wide open, is a tall, yellow-skinned male, known simply as Killer, Smoke's head of security.

"Now um... What's your name?" Smoke asks, with a sweep of the hand. "Naw, Fuck it... Your name doesn't even matter, but
I gotta know... How did you get in my suite!?"

"The, the bedroom window." Tee said, stuttering, complexion almost as white as a prison wall in a two-man cell.

"Listen, listen" Smoke waves his hand, "Please don't start with the scary shit... You should've thought about that before you attempted to rob a multi-million-dollar drug dealer.
Really! I mean really! Did you think I, me" He points to himself, "Damone fucking Jackson! Smoke! Head of the fucking Diry Nine Thieves! Me!" He shouts, with humor, void of all anger. "Would come into a hotel, with five women, and not have all angles covered... You stupid muthafucka!" He states, now eliminating all humor, replacing it with anger hot enough to physically feel. "Most muthafuckas rob banks... Yet in this case, you were better off carjacking Barack and Michelle Obama, killing their kids, holding them ransom, than to even dream about

165

picking up a stack of cash I accidentally dropped... Let alone rob me!"

It's amazing how certain moments in time, you can see how close and yet how far we are from our animal friends. They say dogs can smell fear, and at that very moment, I can believe it. The smell of fear in this room is as strong as the smell of a broken bottle of perfume in a closed closet. The tension is thick enough to slice with a katana blade.

Damone finishes his statement, leaving the room cloaked in silence. Tee and his small army, sitting in a sweet silence, regretting to follow a man with a great vision, but no resemblance of a plan.

"So... This is what is about to happen," Damone said, hands back in his pockets, anger gone. "All of you are going to drop your weapons, and for the first time in a very, very, very long time... I am going to let this shit slide and allow y'all to walk the fuck out of here. Okay?"

With those words, the color starts to ease back into Tee's face and quickly he orders his team to drop their weapons. "Now that's better... Also, why didn't y'all come in shooting? Just curious." asks Smoke, and now I can see why he's as feared as he is. This man standing in front of me has all the qualities of a boss and more. Also, he gives mercy when he doesn't have to.

"We were planning to hold you hostage and the more people, the more money... Sorry." Tee said, attempting to smile.

"Hey, no harm, no foul. Everybody should be as ambitious." He said, as all of Tee's team start to file out, but get blocked by Killer and his team of security.

Tee looks back at Smoke, a questioning expression on his face. Damone's look that he gives Tee, causes once again all the color to drain out of his face.

"Did you really think I was going to let this shit slide?" He deadpans, no emotion in his words. "Mercy is for God, and I am far from being Him... I did not get to the statue I have by being passive and letting the inexcusable slide... Test me and I put my foot so far up your ass the water on your knee will quench your thirst! Yo, Killer... Do what you get paid to do." Immediately, Killer and his team shoved Tee and his team in the room across the hall. The last thing being seen is the butts of rifles hitting heads and people passing out.

"Damn! I hate times like this. Now, I got to call some police I have on my payroll to cover this shit up!" Smoke said, pulling his cellphone out.

I look at Damone Jackson and realize, it's time to tighten up. He's shown me that a real boss, makes executive decisions, letting his team carry them out. Plus, ain't no emotions involved in business, and business isn't just limited to the transfer of products, services, and money from one palm to another. Even death is business, and for the first time, I realize that also extends to the times you aren't paid to do it.

Chapter 14

The dim glow from the almost distinguished candles gives the room an eerie feel that makes Hunter feel at home. Laying in a king-size bed, receiving oral satisfaction from a slim Chinese woman he met while in New York living in one of his many existences. Hunter contemplates the next move in the earthly chest game he plays, yet to use the word contemplate may be too broad of a term, for he definitely knows exactly what the next move is. To be honest, it's a beauty, if he must say so himself.

Looking down at the woman as she swallows his manhood, he finds it amazing how control can come in the oddest of forms. For instance, he thinks about the way, and the why he met Shi'ama.

"Why, aren't you a sight for sore eyes?" Hunter says, approaching Shi'ama in Saks Fifth Avenue. Looking at her, he actually finds the lender Chinese woman quite attractive. The closer he comes to her, he admires her round face shrouded by silky long hair.

He must admit, her breast size could be a lot bigger for his taste, and her ass also. Yet, what she lacks in those areas, she more than makes up for with her beautiful face and gap as wide as the Grand Canyon between her legs.

"You know," She pauses, taking Hunter in with some of the deepest black eyes he has yet to see on a woman. "That's an old line... How often do you use it?"

"Old huh?" Hunter smirks. "Both sight and eyes have been around far longer than the metaphor I used... So for mine to still get sore, I guess that's a compliment for you." "Really!" She said, with a laugh still full of youth despite her age, which Hunter knows to be thirty-seven. "What you just said made no sense at all... But it was cute."

"Oh, it made more sense than you may think," replies Hunter, as one of the many workers comes along, handing Shi'ama a red dress that has to cost somewhere in the range of five thousand dollars.

"Is that so? Explain... I'm intrigued." She said while handing the dress back to the woman, without so much as looking at it.

"Hmm." Hunter pauses for effect, "It's simple... What I said was a metaphor followed by another metaphor as an answer. For we both know that eyes do not get sore by merely gazing upon people, but with time... So."

"You were only stating that you are old and wasn't complimenting me in the least!" Shi'ama snaps, with a dead serious look on her face.

Staring at her, Hunter is laughing inside. He knew his approach, his answer, and her realization would lead up to this moment.

Moving his gaze behind, as not to burst into a fit of laughter, he calms this feeling by thinking about the pedestal he sits on while the rest of the ants run in circles below him.

In Shi'ama's mind, it's impossible for any man to deny the fact she's beautiful. True, if that man only stepped to her on a purely physical impulse, yet in Hunter's case, he has

169

mastered the physical. Every move in life has a meaning to get one step closer to the end. So, before this moment, unbeknownst to Shi'ama, he took her through a six-month observation process, just as he does all his chest pieces.

While she lived her life, Hunter has been her waiter, the bellhop at the five-star hotel she sneaks into to cheat on her husband, and a plethora of other characters in her life she's passed in her day-to-day activities, yet never even noticed. God, it's amazing! He thinks to himself. How the sheep never sees the wolf until it's too late.

"Really, you mustn't take my statement as an insult." He smiles.

"Hmmf!" She snorts, with an attitude that gets a slight chuckle out of Hunter. "Listen," He continues to smile. "I know you're used to most men being in some form of awe by your timeless beauty, and status in like, but that doesn't app—"

"You!" Shi'ama shouts, "Know nothing about me!"

"Really?" Hunter raises his eyebrows while maintaining his smiling face. "Well, let's see... You're Shi'ama Yamasuta, wife of multimillionaire Chan Yamasuta... You crave love and attention, why? Because you're lonely, with a husband in the technology industry, you're tired of hearing gigabyte this...
Gigabyte that... Am I close?"

"How? How do you know so much about me?" Shi'ama looks at him with a bewildered look on her face, clutching the front of her blouse.

For Hunter, this is the most exhilarating moment of this whole encounter. This is the moment of control. He knew, just as with most vain humans, Shi'ama was no exception to the rules... To destroy the confidence, you must first lower them to nothing. The insult... Show them they're insignificant, the intel... Build them back up to a false reality.

"How do I know so much about you?" He said, lowering his voice, stepping close enough that Shi'ama can feel the next words he says on the nape of her neck.

"You've been my obsession since I saw you on the red carpet at the inspiring minds even six months ago. Standing you were, next to your husband... I saw you; I saw a woman lonely, drowning in the deep water of despair."

Shi'ama's body almost goes limp as Hunter whispers her life problems into her ear. Pulling her closer, Hunter continues to build his fortress of control.

"But Shi'ama, I'm here to tell you, you're more than a nice arm piece to flaunt at parties. Only to be left home when your body needs to be pleasured. Shi'ama, you're a sight for old eyes because your beauty is timeless, yet..." He pauses, cupping her chin in his hand. "I'm here for you... To pleasure you... To love you and only you." He said, looking into her eyes, lightly brushing his lips against hers, catching her as her knees weaken, unable to hold her weight.

"Oh... Oh my God." Shi'ama pants, with an all-familiar shudder Hunter's seen so many times.

"Um, Ma'am... Ma'am." She signals a store clerk.

"Yes, Mrs. Yamasuta." Says the store clerk.

"I would like to look at your best selection of thongs." She said, backing up, looking Hunter in the eyes. "I've just soiled mine..."

Hunter comes back to the moment with a bark of laughter, as he remembers watching Shi'ama's love juices slide down the inside of her leg.
"What's so funny?" She asks, hand still clutching his manhood.

"Nothing... Nothing at all."

"Well... Would you please hurry up and cum! My jaws are starting to hurt baby! Forty-five minutes is a long time!"

"No problem." He said, pulling her up into his arms.

"No... No... I've cum at least five times already, it's only right."

"It's fine, we've got to talk... Did you do what I asked?"

"Of course! But I can't see why telling my husband about you is so important, Neiros!"

"Well, baby" Hunter smiles, "Sometimes... You have to paint the picture in the most colorful way possible in order to make someone see the obvious."

"If you say so... I also got that banking info you wanted as well."

"Now, that," Hunter said, while getting out of the bed. "Is perfect."

"So... Are we still going to do this together? I never thought I'd ever consider robbing my husband and run—" Shi'ama stops mid-sentence, as Hunter flips her over, straddling her.

"Oh... Baby! You're ready to go again!"

"More than you know." He replies, placing a handheld camera to his eye, grabbing Shi'ama around the neck. "Oh... Neiros, I like it kinky, baby!... Baby! Ba—" She starts to struggle in an attempt to get out of Hunter's iron grip.

"Baby! Please... Stop! I, I, can't..." Hunter smiles as she starts kicking and scratching him trying to get loose.

Once again, this is one of the moments... One of the controlling moments. He watches with an uncontrollable urge to laugh as Shi'ama turns deep blue, her tongue hanging out of her mouth, eyes bulging out of their sockets... The moment, the defining moment of ultimate control.

Hunter ejaculates as all the life seeps out of Shi'ama's body, like a balloon with a slow leak, cursing himself for cumming on her body.

"That's life." He says, turning the camera off,
picking Shi'ama's lifeless corpse up, dropping it in the tub, turning on the water to its hottest temperature, then pouring a gallon of bleach in the water.

Putting on a pair of latex gloves, he places the videotape in an envelope, getting ready to send it to Shi'ama's husband, who despite being the owner of a tech firm, he is also an underboss in the Chinese mafia.

Stripping the room of all evidence leading to himself, he laughs, thinking Chan is going to be one pissed-off chink, waking up one hundred million dollars poorer, with a dead wife to boot. All curtesy of Neiros Simmons. But hey, if the student can't excel the teacher, what good is he?

***

I spent time with Damone, and the crazy part is shit has been quiet as fuck. Which is never a good thing, in my life, to be honest, I've had too much shit going on for things to just die the fuck down, but sometimes shit happens in the strangest ways. So, being me, I went back to work. About a week ago, I got a contract on this one tycoon giving out in Texas. Some fat, rich, white dude that just so happened to piss his wife off. But the thing is, I can't just snipe the fucker. I've got to make it look like more than a hit, which was a lot easier than I thought.

Sitting in a restaurant in the higher maintenance section of Dallas. I waited until he came to meet one of his many mistresses. As I walk into the restaurant, the Mai'tre O looks at me with a peculiar look, yet what the fuck did I expect. Looking around earlier, there were only about six, maybe seven African Americans in the place. So I had to make reservations and once he saw my name on the list, he eased up somewhat. Once inside, I spot my target in the far corner of the place with his date's back to me, and oh shit! This cracka got a thang for sisters! I see why he's creeping.

Setting back into my own table, I look around at the finely decorated establishment. Now, I am not into the whole art scene, yet I can tell the paintings on the wall cost a pretty penny. Even the silverware in this place is high priced. Picking up the menu, I start putting my plan together. The way I see it, once they get their check, I'll go to the bathroom, change clothes, rob him, the parking attendant, and his bitch, killing them all. Gotta make it look good.

"Oh! Somebody help! Please, he's choking!" said an all too familiar voice, bringing me out of my thoughts.

I watch as someone comes to my target's aid, giving him the Heimlich maneuver and to my surprise, Sienna stands next to him with crocodile tears down her face.

Ain't this some shit! Now how this bitch done pulled this shit off! But damn, I must admit, she got this shit on lock. Standing by the crowd of on-lookers in a body-fitting dress, slowly inching her way away.

What the fuck! Did this bitch just wink at me? Oh... I got something for her ass! Quickly, I slide out of the booth I'm in, heading for the exit. Just as I thought, once I get past all the distraught customers, I catch Sienna coming out of an alleyway on the side of the building.

It's dark out, but I can make out the silhouette of her fine ass, as she strides down the street at a leisurely pace. Coming up beside her, I lightly touch her elbow.

"So... What brings you way out this way?"

"The same thing that brought you out this way." She answers, stopping, and turning towards me, giving me one of them sarcastic looks of hers, but damn! This bitch smells good!

"Chanel." She said, reading my thoughts.

"What?" I act stupid.

"My parfum... Chanel."

"Yeah," I said, trying to feign non-interest, knowing that right now, everything about her for some reason is turning me the fuck on! "Well, fuck that... What the fuck are you doing here!"

"Who? Me?" She flutters her eyes while placing her hand against the breast "Oh... I'm just fulfilling a contract... Why?"

"That was my mark."

"Oh, I know, but even though we've called a truce as to killing one another, I decided there can't be two great assassins in this business... Only one." She turns away, walking down another alley.

I stand in the muggy night, watching my ex-wife turned nemesis, saunter off, and I decided to act on my first impulse. I take pursuit as soon as she passes a dumpster. I push her facefirst into the wall with just enough force not to hurt her, pulling her tight dress up to her waist.

"Neiros! What are you doing?" She said in a husky voice.

"Finishing our conversation," I replied, unzipping my pants, bending her over at the waist.

Sienna lets out a light grunt as I slam into her unbelievably wet honey pot.

"So" I start, pulling her long, silky hair, sticking her from behind. "You wanna be the best? How can that be and you can't even beat me at something as simple as sex?"

"I... Uh... I... Uh, uh... Get to differ!" She finally gets out, suddenly pulling away from me, in the same motion grabbing me by my suit jacket, with the ease of a professional martial artist. Sienna puts me on my back, the next thing I know, she's riding me, vaginal muscles squeezing and loosening on my manhood, threatening to bring me over the edge.

"Now... What was that comment you made about not being able to beat you? Come on... Cum for momma." She coos, and this side of my wife I've never seen... Ever, but as much as this shit is turning me on: I can't let this bitch win.

At the right moment, I flip her over onto the alley floor. Looking around, I see coke cans, and other debris scattered everywhere. The smell of garbage, Chinese food, and raw sexual musk linger in the air. This may be the dirtiest time I've had with my wife, yet it's also the most interesting.

As I pound into Sienna, I look into her eyes, knowing I'm going to win this battle. Victory is written all over her face, as she bites her lips, keeping her eyes closed in an effort to stop the orgasm on the edge of the cliff.

"Don't fight it Si... Let it go, cum for me baby."

"I... I won't" she said, desperation thick in her words.

"Yes, you will."

"No!" She shouts, and the bitch bites me on the neck so hard, I ease back. Which is enough for her to get away, pinning me on my back.

"Oh, no you won't!" I exclaim, seeing her trying to put my meat in her mouth. "That's cheating!"

"No... It's—" Sienna starts to say, cut off by the sound of boots not even two feet from my head. Looking up, the expression on her face is one of happiness and confusion.

"Uncle!" She exclaims, my manhood still in her clutch.

I look up and I'm not happy at all but shocked.

"Hunter!" I said, looking up at my mentor/father/enemy in one.

"Really children?" He smiles. "Stop playing in the filth... We have a lot to talk about."

After getting dressed, we follow Hunter to a seedy motel. Sitting in his room, the only thoughts going through my mind is: How the fuck? When does it stop?

This nigga never seems to reach his stopping point. Just as you think you know all there is to think about him, something else pops the fuck up!

178

Watching him and Sienna catch up on old memories, shows me how much I could not know. All this time, I've never even entertained the possibility of Hunter even knowing my wife, let alone being her uncle.

"Hold the fuck up!" I yell, out of frustration, "You're her fucking uncle! How in the fuck!"

"Neiros," Hunter said, calmy. "One of your flaws is you've tended to look too much into your own life instead of examining the lives of the ones around you."

"Bullshit!" I exclaim while standing, starting to pace back and forth. "Not one time has she even mentioned you or have you even men..." I cut myself short, as it downs on me. The reason I never noticed the connection was in part because she never mentioned him, nor did he mention her, but I also never asked my wife about her family. I never really cared about meeting them.
This may sound crazy, but outside of Sienna's mother and father, I don't know any of her family. Yeah, she's mentioned a brother and I think a sister. But, "Oh... It's finally hit you huh?" Hunter said, with a smug grin on his face. "You don't even know the woman you've married and impregnated... Hmf! Ain't that some shit huh... Well, that is about to change, dramatically... As you both know as of late, someone has been paying assassins to kill the ones close to them."

"That's been you," Sienna said, shock in her voice.
"Well," he shrugs "Me and a few friends."

"But why?" I ask.

"Really... Boredom, but that's just part one... In about, ummm... 18 hours, you both, along with some other teams will be getting a text to team up and hunt another team."

"You can't be serious!" exclaims Sienna, "You're telling me that just for shits and giggles... You—" Sienna is cut short, as I dive on her in time to stop the sniper's bullet from piercing her brain. Luckily for her, I saw the moonlight flicker off the scope in time.

Just as the pillow by her head explodes, an assault of bullets rains into the room. Coming around to the side of our bed, Hunter hunkers down with this silly ass grin on his face. Just as a bullet slams into the little 12" T.V., sending glass everything. "18 hours!" I yell in my face.

"Oh! My bad." He yells. "I meant 18 hours as of yesterday!" It seems as if the assault of bullets continues for what seems like hours, yet is only a minute or two. Afterwards, the silence is deafening. "Wel... That's my cue." Hunter said, the sound of police sirens beginning to be heard in the distance, growing louder the closer they get. "Well, you kids take care! You should be straight."

"Hold up!" I stand up. "Who the fuck was that!"

"You should've gotten a message by now... They just got theirs first." Hunter says, just as he finishes his statement, the phone in my back pocket starts to play 2-RO's "These niggas."

"Jizzle," I say, keeping my eyes on a smiling Hunter. For some reason, this muthafucka always gets a kick out of the most intense situations.

"Hey... It's Tavis... Um, you've got a contract." states Tavis, but the tone of his voice isn't the same as it normally is.

"Yeah... I'm sure my mark has a contract out on me, being that they just got finished shooting up the motel I'm in... So, who is it?"

"The marks are two assassins... A mother and a daughter team out of Switzerland. That only go by the names Night and Day... They are also paid to off you and the thing is... Nobody's actually seen them."

"Well... Two white bitches ain't going to be that much of a problem Tavis... So, who is the contractor?" I ask, knowing the answer, but wanting to hear Tavis say it.

"Come on Death... You know I'm not going to tell you that."

"Well, shits been crazy lately... I had to try."

"Tell Tavis I'm here and he can tell you all you would like to know."

"Tavis." I start, wondering what else Hunter has up his sleeve.

"Do you know a man by the name of Hunter?"

"Ummm, yeah...Why?" He timidly answers.

"He's here... And said to tell you to tell me what I want to know."

Tavis's pause on the other end of the line warns me this is not one I'm going to be ready for. The crazy thing is, the way I met this, I shouldn't have any form of attachment to him, but it's been years since that steamy night in Miami......
Sitting at a bar, drinking a Hennessey on the rocks, I think to myself that maybe this record label shit ain't as easy as I once thought it was. When this big ass white dude, about 6"7', at least 260 lbs., taps me on the shoulder.

"Yeah," I said, turning around to stare into the eyes of the blue-eyed, blond-haired monster.

"You're sitting in my seat boy!" He said, leaning into me. Here's the thing, his first mistake was leaning too close to my knee with his front open to me. If he had turned sideways, maybe this would've been more of a challenge, but then again, I think as I take notice that there are about six more dudes with the same characteristics as the one in front of me, staring in our direction. This may be harder than I once thought.

At first, I thought this was some racist shit. Then I took notice that about two of them were sitting at a table with some black men, yet once I noticed how they had themselves positioned, I saw they had put me in a box, on some military-type shit.

So, being wise, I smile and say, "My bad man." Starting to get up, yet this dude doesn't move.

"It ain't going to be that easy boy... The only way I can let this go is if you pay me and my brothers a small fee." He cracks his knuckles, smiling.

"How small a fee?"

"For you... Twenty grand should do."

"Twenty grand, huh?"

This cracka got me fucked up! Granted in his mind, he has this shit mapped out, but he's doing the one thing no man should ever do, and that's to underestimate your mark.
Now, I know his plan is to get me to go to the bank and get these funds. Maybe he thinks I'm a dopeboy with twenty grand close by. I don't know, yet granted both of his probable assumptions are true in a sense. The one thing he didn't factor in his plans, I'm a certified killer and I'll be damned if this fuck ass cracka is going to take shit from Jizzle.

"Well, sir... Today just so happens to be your lucky day." I said, watching the smile on his face widen. "I don't want no trouble, and to be honest, I'm not from here. So, if you'll follow me to my car... I'm pretty sure we can solve this situation without violence."

"You know boy... Sometimes you niggers ain't as dumb as I always say you are." He said while patting my shoulder.

"Yeah," I respond, with a weak smile, meant to come off as nervous.

Standing up, this is when all the training Hunter has given comes to the front of my brain. The moment I step out of the stool, everything slows down. The first thing I notice is the waitress walking towards me.

The look on her face tells me she's seen the man

accompanying me more than once. So they do this a lot, with a quick sweep of the head, I place the positions of all of the possible accomplices into my photographic memory. Walking towards the door, I realize something is off. He's not walking as close to me as he should. Most predators of his kind, tend to walk close to their victims in order to stop them from making a swift getaway.

Once we're outside, on the side of the bar, he steps in closer, just as the rest of his team comes out the side door of the bar. This is the moment I've been anticipating, the alleyway is dark, due to the moonless sky. So these men may not be able to notice me.

Yep. They never notice the .22 caliber pistol I slide out of my pocket, from what I can tell, they're about fifty feet from my position. So now is the time. With an abrupt stop and a swift elbow, I totally catch the man behind me off guard.

The moment he clutches his throat, the others start to run towards me, lifting the pistol, I let about three shots go, hitting two of them, starting my spin as the other four pull out pistols, starting to shoot.

My timing is perfect, the man behind me stands up, becoming a shield for the many bullets racing my way, giving me enough time to unholster my .45, getting behind a dumpster. I can hear the shells hitting the ground, as the men came to a stop, moving slowly towards my position.

The only thing I focus on is the sound of their footsteps, the smell of their cologne getting closer and closer as they kept coming.

"Did any of y'all see where he went?" One of them questions.

"No... but that nigger is going to pay for what he did to Ice!" Another one threatened, with what sounds like tears in his voice.

"Damn! Do you think he's dead?" Asks another man

"It sure looks like it."

They continue down the alleyway debating about Ice's condition. In that time, I use it to peek around the dumpster to see how they are arranged. Once I lock their position into my mind, I grab a nearby can, tossing it as far behind them as I can.

My plan works like a charm, the moment the can hits the ground, just as I assumed they would, all four of them spun completely around, pistols down, giving me the perfect moment to slide from behind the dumpster, still ducked low, letting off six shoots, taking all four of the men out. Honestly, I was somewhat upset. That shit was entirely too damn easy.

As I stand up, reholstering my pistol, a man comes walking into the alleyway clapping. You know one of them is sarcastic, clap... Clap... Clap... Type of shits.

"Wow." He said, once I spun around, pistole drawn. "Chill, just chill." He holds both his hands up." I mean you no harm"

"That's good...But who the fuck are you?" I said, looking at the 4'9" white male, it's somewhat hard to tell, but from the small amount of light he's standing in, I think he is brown, maybe black, but I can tell he's wearing a pair of wire-rim glasses and a nice suit.

"Who, me?"

"No! The muthafuckin white man about to die!" I train my gun on him.

"Listen, listen man... My name is Tavis... Tavis Teams, and I sort of set this situation up."

"Oh, so you the one that got these crackas killed for nothing!"

"Pretty much!"

"Why?"
"Well... One" He counts his fingers. "They use to pick on me when I was in high school... And two: I've been sent to recruit you. Death. Hey! Hey! Hey!" He yells when I rush forward, putting my pistol in the middle of his forehead.

"Recruit me for what and how the fuck do you know me by that name!"

"Aw shit!" Tavis sighs. "I was told this wasn't going to be easy, but damn! Listen here, my bosses are contractors for people who want people dead. You're good, but I can make you untraceable... I've been on your trail since the Groni hit. One may I add was damn good, but you could've done better on the Teddy G. Hit... I'm just saying." He shrugs. "Bottom line, my people want you and are willing to pay top dollar for your services."

The wind started to pick up, bringing up the smell of rain along for the ride. Which reminded me, I was standing in an alley, with seven dead bodies, and a pistol in the face of a white boy, who looks like he's part of corporate America.

"oh... Don't worry about the police." Tavis reads my thought going in his pocket pulling out a small computer. "About seven people have called the police, all of their calls have been forwarded by my ten-mile scrambler." He said, cocky ass grin on his face, just then, an all-white van pulled up and out jumps a team of at least seven men. "oh don't worry, they're here to clean up... Sam, Tony, I need y'all to make this..." Tavis waves his hand, "disappear. So, are you in or out?"

"Well," Tavis says, after his lengthy pause. "one of the contractors is in the room with you, and that would be Hunter... Another one is on the phone with you" He states, his statement sending my mind into shock. Tavis! A contractor!
How the fuck!

"You're probably questioning how and why... So let's job the memory of yours... About six months before I met you... You did the Teddy G hit... With him was this cute little redbone by the name of Avery... Huh... What? Got your tongue... Figures...well, my mother's second husband was a black man. Yeah, you piece of shit! YOU KILLED MY SISTER! The only way I was able to find you was because my mother's second husband's name was Terrance Hunter!"

I hear the words coming out of Tavis' mouth, but it's Hunter's smug lack that's got my full attention. "What..." Tavis starts to say, but I hung the phone up.

For about a minute, I just stare at Hunter as it all downs on me, all of this time, all my life, my wife, and all this, has just been a part of some sick game. All set up by the man in front of me.

"So." I said, trying to hold my composure, "All this time...all this time...you've been playing me like a chess piece?"

The gesture that hunter makes almost forces me to lose all control, standing just across the bullet-ridden bed, he looks off to the side, as if I'm not important enough to entertain, saying

"Maybe some other time." he dashes out the door. I jump over the bed, hitting the door, just as the first police cruiser comes pilling into the parking lot. At the same time, my phone rings.

"Hunter!" I yell, with a little too much force.

"No, no... It's Tivia, Neiros."

"Not now Tivia!"

"Yes now, Jizzle."

"What! What is so important it can't wait?"

"Somebody burnt the studio down!"

Chapter 15

"Jizzle! Jizzle! Jizzle!" Tivia yells. Into a dead phone.

After attempting to call back about three times, she hangs up, looking over at the charred remains that once held so many memories for her, but now is just a skeleton of its old self.

"Tivia!" Akeema says, walking up. "Did you get in touch with your boss?"

"Yeah yeah. But he must be going through some other shit. Because he just hung the phone up." Tivia answers, still thinking about Jizzle's actions. Which strikes her as odd. One of the attributes he possesses, that she admires about him, is he can remain utterly calm under pressure. There has been plenty of times she really thought he was going to explode, but he would still keep his cool despite the bullshit that was going on. What the fuck is going on?

"Do you have any idea who would do this?" Asks Akeema as a black limo comes to a stop in front of them.

Both Tivia and Akema take a step back, as the driver emerges, walking around to open the back door, "Get in." He says in a dead voice.

"No." Tivia shakes her head. "We good."

"Ladies... I mean you no harm..." Said a voice from within.

"Please... Just a moment of your time."

Tivia and Akema look at each other Timidly before agreeing to get in. Once they were inside, the first person they see is a small Chinese man seating in the far corner of the luxurious vehicle. From the looks of it, one would swear they were in a small apartment, minus a bedroom.

The purple lighting aluminates the white leather to an almost glow. Tivia looks over, sees the small mini-bar, equipped with the mini-fridge, and thinks, Damn. Buddy paid!

That becomes an understatement once she sees the back of six T.V. screens, realizing that only one of them is for entertainment purposes. The rest for cameras positioned at various points of the car. 'Sit ladies." says the Chinaman.

"Sorry to just pop up, but this is one of the most urgent businesses... Do you work for a Mr. Neiros Simmons?"

"That all depends," responds Tivia.

"On?"

"Why are you asking?"

"Well... That is a somewhat answer to my question. My reason is I would like to speak with him personally about something, and I thought you would be more than willing to assist me, but since we must do it my way... Yiatshi!" exclaims the man, the middle portion parting exposing a beautiful oriental woman, who with the speed of a water moccasin strikes Tivia and Akeema with tranquilizing darts.

"Aw shit! Not again!" Tivia shit, before everything goes black.

Two blocks away, Flow cruises through Jacksonville listening to the Watch the Thrown, disc by Jay-Z and Kanye West, singing along with Niggaz in Paris. He reflects on the differences between the south and the north.

In his opinion, the streets only differ as it pertains to product and the way niggaz go about moving the shit. For him, it wasn't coke and weed as the main product of choice, but heroin.

Growing up in Queens, at the young age of twelve, he was on the block in the cold with a bundle of blue tops in his Triple Goose, high-grade weed in his front pocket, and a .45 in his back pocket. Walking down 151st, trying to survive. Down here, niggas on this cellphone game. Where he came from, when the phone rang, it was only fam or pussy. Mostly pussy in his case.

One thing he didn't have to worry about was pussy! Being 6", pure Dominican, with long natural hair, women would damn near sell their souls for just a moment of his time. Looking around at the littered streets, he sees the other difference between him and them. Even at a young age, Flow's main focus was money and hoes. He was never the type to be on that murder shit, but don't get it twisted, if need be, he'll body something quick. Actually, that's why he had to leave Deltona and come live with his homebody Damone...

Sitting in his living room playing NBA2k, Flow looks over at the Venezuelan/Puerto Rican beauty he just pounded to sleep. Watching Mona sleep, he can't help but get aroused just looking at her size C breast rising and falling. Even in her sleep, her facial expression had that 'come fuck me look on it. Flow completely forgets about the video game, continuing to visually travel down her flat stomach, only to stop at her luscious honey pot, fat enough to be considered two, but he knows it's pubic hairs that give it that effect.

As if his gaze has a physical effect, Mona opens her eyes, staring at him with some of the most beautiful brown, flaked with hazel eyes he's seen.

"What Papi?" says her angelic voice.

"Nothing... Just admiring your beauty," responds Flow, putting his attention back on the game. Only to notice he's been violated twice for shot clock violations.

"You know what?" Mona says, now on the sofa with him, hands on his shoulders.

"What?" He answers as she starts to rub his chest making her way down to his already erected manhood.

"You say the nicest things about me."

"I'm just the truthful type ma." Flow puts the game on pause, as she frees him, stroking him in long, slow strokes. "But shit, you can always show me how good I make you feel."

"Anytime Papi," Mona says, with the skill of a pornstar, engulfing him totally without gagging. Flow watches, amazed and in absolute bliss, as she slows down, popping him out, only to run her tongue from the tip to the bottom of his shaft, slowly slicking back up. Engulfing him again, then speeding up her motion, giving it to him just how he likes it. Sloppy and wet.

Leaning his head back, enjoying Mona's skills, he's totally oblivious of the fact someone has crept into the living room, finding out only when Mona screams bloody murder.

"Caught yo fuck ass slipping pretty boy ass chico!" exclaims the masked gunman. "Yeah, gone head! Put ya dick back in yo pants! Slowly nigga!" The man said, showing signs of nervousness.

Slowly, Flow gets up after doing as commanded, looking the man in the eyes. One of the main lessons all older Kings taught him that still rings true to this day is the fact that the eyes are the window to the soul, and looking into the eyes of this would be jackboy, he can tell this nigga is a lot more scared than he should be.

"Alright! Enough of this stare-me-down shit! Where the cash at?" The masked man shouts, shaking his pistol at Flow.

"Listen nigga, I ain't got shit for ya. You gone have to search this bitch ya damn self!" Flow said, pulling off a bold move, sitting down.

"Oh! Oh! You think this shit is sweet!" The man points the gun at Mona. "Get that cash up or I'll off this bitch!"

"Ha!" Flow laughs, "Nigga, I don't give a fuck about that bitch! And to be honest, I think you too pussy to merc anything up in this bitch!" Flow leans forward, grabbing a prerolled blunt he had meant to smoke earlier. Looking at the masked man, he whales deeply, exhaling, blowing a stream of smoke in the man's direction.

In his mind, as he picks the game controller up, he knows he shouldn't be taunting any man with a loaded gun. Plus, even though in theory, he doesn't care enough about Mona to put her before the money. Because, pussy is like a weed in Jamaica, what you can't find on the side of the road, you can buy, but she is a good girl. So he doesn't want the man to kill her, yet in this case, he knows his confident demeanor is fucking with the man's thought process.

Flow's demeanor doesn't change in the least as he rushes up to Mona, who by this point has tears running down that beautiful face of hers, grabbing a fistful of her hair, pressing the pistol to her forehead.

Flow almost grimaces, he knows Mona is going to have a mark on that beautiful face of hers by the amount of force he's using to press the gun against her forehead, but now he has somewhat of a chance.

The problem with amateur jack boys is this. There is no way in hell you should ever leave the threat with enough distance between you and him, to do what Flow is about to do.

As the man declares, "You got ten seconds to get that cash up!"

This gives Flow just enough time to ease his hand inside the chair he's sitting in, pulling out one of the many guns he's stashed around the apartment.

The man's eyes get as big as a fifty-cent piece when Flow pulls the gun up. At that moment, he doesn't realize it, but the game is over. Because at this point he has two options: 1. kill Mona or 2. Shoot at Flow who is across the living room on the move. Either way, the odds of him coming out of this situation as a winner, are slim to none.

Choosing his last option, he fires a wild shot at Flow, just as he dives sideways. The bullet missing him, hitting the center of the chair, which is crazy enough, would've been a fatal wound.

Flow rolls behind the sofa, crawling towards the hallway, just as a piece of plaster burst free from the wall behind his head. Damn! Flow thinks to himself. This nigga is a better shooter than I thought!

Allowing his breathing to slow, he peeks around the corner, watching as the masked man ducks behind the sofa. Waiting for him to come out, Flow calmly looks around for something bulky. Only to find Mona's backpack.
Grabbing it, he tosses it in the air, knowing the nervous Jack Boy would do exactly what he does. Starts to fire at the pack until his gun empties. Standing up, Flow walks into the living room where the man has Mona in a chokehold.

"Back up! Back up! I'll snap this bitch's neck!" He said, wetting the mask covering his face with his spit.

Flow looks Mona in the eyes, hating himself for what he knows he must do. As much as he would love to spare her, he knows he can't. He's definitely going to murder this man, and the truth of the matter is, dead people cannot place their hands on the Bible in court.

The moment Mona realizes what is about to happen, she immediately starts to struggle in the man's hold. "Papi no!

Please, Papi!" She screams, getting a start out of the man, causing him to realize Flow's intentions.

"Oh shit!" he backs, tossing Mona to the side, trying to get to the door. The masked man comes very short of escaping as Flow's pistol barks fire, pushing small pieces of lead into the back of his body. Leaving nasty exit wounds as they exit out the front forcing him to land his face first on the living room floor.

Walking up, Flow places two more shots into the man's head, turning around to take Mona out, to find her vigorously cleaning.

At first, he thinks the girl has lost her mind until he realizes she's wiping every surface free of prints.

"Mona! Mona!" Flow drops his head.

"You're wasting your time."
"Please Papi! Please! Give me a chance! I promise I won't say anything." she stares, eyes frantic, steadily wiping.

"So... What is your plan?" Flow scratches his head with the pistol.

"I wipe everything down... And call the police and tell them he tried to rape me, but I got away, and in a fit of rage killed him."

"What about me?"

"I don't know you. This is my apartment. If the police ask why it's in your name, I'll just tell them a friend of mine who's gone now, had it put in your name!"

Damn! Flow thinks to himself. That'll work, especially due to the fact the apartment is in some female baser's name he paid fifty dollars.

"That's what it do." He said, starting to pack, calling Damone, leaving Mona twenty grand for her troubles.

***

Those two weeks seemed like years ago. Flow comes back to the present, thinking about how his life is about to take a turn for the better. Once he got to Jacksonville, he had fifty stacks to his name and his car, but Damone, a longtime friend of his, he met through one of his childhood friends C.J., stepped up the plate and for half of what he came to the city with, gave him three kilos of cocaine and a spot to move into. Someplace on the outskirts of Jacksonville called Middleburg.

Now, all he's waiting for is Damone to let him know who to off the shit to and it's on and poppin.
"Bout time yo pretty boy ass came round this bitch to see me." Smiles C.J. "I was about to come find yo ass and kick it!" He taunts as Flow pulls up.

C.J. one of Flows, well Flow's only mentor, is a Dominican and Black twenty-eight-year-old ex-convict, who caught two life sentences at the age of fourteen, and it took fourteen years to give it back. They met in one of the many institutions in Florida. When Flow caught a small bid for

197

carjacking at the age of eighteen, from the moment they met, they hit it off.

By that time, C.J. had been down for a minute, was past the wild stage in his life. While Flow was just starting his, yet due
to C.J.'s patience with him, he was able to slow down. Once C.J. got out, he maintained contact with Flow until the day he walked out of the gates.

"Nigga, you ain't gone do shit to me! If anything, I'll kick yo ass!"

"Yeah... Anybody can dream...So, what's good which ya?" C.J. embarrasses Flow in a hug.

"Same shit... You know me, money and hoes."

"Yeah... That's yo problem now... But you thought about what we talked about?" C.J. refers to Flow going legit with him.

"Yeah... I thought about it."

"And?"

"Damone just put me on, brah."

"You gone make me kick both you and Damone's ass!"

"Shit! Me and Damone bumping nigga! The fuck you mean!" "Whateva... Listen, I understand you got the whole little stretch shit going... That's cool, but that shit ain't gone last forever... Yo ass gone end up in prison... Again! And I'm not gonna come and break you out. Just to kick yo ass!"

"You damn sho talk about kicking my ass a lot."

"Because I know I can."

"You think you can."

"Now... Trust me, all this anger I got built up in me... Just a small bit of release and you'll go screaming for help." C.J. mimics Flow running for help.

"Fuck you... But, on the real... I'll think about it." answers Flow, as his cellphone rings. "Damone... What's up?"

"Good news... You straight?"

"Yeah... I'm with C.J."

"Yo! Tell him I said fuck him!"

"Yo, C.J... Damone said, Fuck you!" Flow says, getting a laugh out of C.J. "What's good?"

"Listen, instead of Middleburg... I got a better situation for you."

"And that is?"

"How about you sliding back up north, with enough dog food to feed the kennel."

"Damn." Flow looks at C.J., knowing that as of this moment, a legitimate life is a thing of the past.

Chapter Seventeen

It's been weeks since Consuela decided to take Hamzah's advice and enroll into F.C.C.J's G.E.D. program. At first, she was somewhat afraid to find out exactly how intelligent she was. Yet to her surprise, she pretty much aced the practice test after studying for a day or two. Then she did even better on the pre G.E.D. test.

Once her teacher Mr. Simmons saw her scores, he immediately decided to put her on the next G.E.D. testing list in the coming six months. So, now Consuela only shows up to work on her writing skills so she can get a better score on the real test.

Being honest with herself, at first, she wanted to quit and just run away from the whole school experience altogether. One of the reasons she hated school before was because of the same hatred she received from females whose boyfriends couldn't help but turn their heads as she walked by. The thing is, she wasn't wearing anything tight or revealing. On the advice of Hamzah, who told her one night... ***

"Hamzah... Can I ask you a question?"

"Feel free to ask away." He answered, staring out into the stormy night.

"Well, the first question is... Why do you spend so much time looking out that window?"

"Because I'm Muslim... and Allah says in the Quran; to ponder his creation, and that in which he created."

"Okay... So?"

"Well take tonight... Allah says in the Quran how he allows the rain to fall in due measure... not too much... not too little... Well, if one was to study the science behind that statement. He would find out that the clouds hold millions of gallons of water in the air, only letting some of it out, but even with all that water suspended in mid-air, a plane can fly completely through it... so, when man studies and contemplates the Quran, he finds out that all the things spoken of, as it pertains to nature, have been proven by science. There is no way possible for an illiterate merchant to have known these things, proving the Quran came from God... What's your next question?" "Oh... Why do Muslim women have to wear all that stuff?" Consuela frowns her face up.

"Ha! Ha!" Hamzah laughs, "The hijab, that's an easy one, from the time you were a child, most men were attracted to your body... Why is that?"

"I don't know... I guess cause I look good!" answers Consuela, getting up, strutting her stuff. Which only makes Hamzah shake his head. "How did they know you looked good? Because, at a young age, you and all of your peers were wearing clothes hat showed the world your shape...due to this, a lot of you were raped, persuaded to have sex at a young age, or forced into the life you just left...the hijab slows that process down... Consuela, yes you are beautiful, and any man would be blessed to have the chance to wake up next to you for the rest of his life. He should want you for more than the physical, that has a slight chance of happening, if the first time he sees you, all the mystery is gone, and the only thought in his mind is to sleep with you. That is just some of the wisdom of the hijab."

*** Consuela is pulled from her memory of a man she's grown to admire in just the short time she's been living with him, by one of the many boys who find it a must to try and talk to her.

"Hey beautiful," says Devan, a 6'1" chocolate-skin man, about the age of nineteen. Devon has been on her trail since the first day he met her, you could say it was love at first sight.

"Hey." She answers, without so much as looking up. It isn't that she doesn't find Devon attracted, with his shortcut and dimples. It's just that she doesn't have the time to even consider having a boyfriend.

"Listen, you ain't got to be all stuck up to me. I understand I ain't the type of guy you're into, being I ain't got stacks and all."

"Please!" Consuela thinks to herself, that's the last type of man she wants. All of the ballers at the school only know how to try to impress her with the one thing she's definitely not in need of and when that doesn't work, their next words are, "Shit!... I'll pay for it!"

That is the last type of man that will get her attention, but to Devon's accusation, she says nothing, continuing to listen. He's allowed to think what he wants. It isn't like she plans on talking to him anyway.

"But..." He pauses. "We can still be friends... I mean, there is a Young Money concert coming up on the 27th of next month and I was wondering, would you like to go with me?" He said, and Consuela can't help but find his timidness cute.

"I" She starts to answer but is cut short by one of the many females that hate on her just because, and this one goes by the name of Angela. She's the worst of the bunch.

Standing 4'3" tall, with a short Halle Berry type cut, she is really no match for Consuela as it pertains to looks, but her body is a totally different story. Angela has one of them onion asses. You know the kind that can make a grown man cry, and from the looks of her thighs, you can tell she does a lot of squats, by the way, they just seem to curve forward away from her ass down to calves that are just the right size, ending at perfect little feet. "Dee!" She said, "Why you over there sweating a dead issue when you can have this?" She runs her hands over her flat stomach up to her size B breast. "I'm good," answers Devan, looking back at Consuela, awaiting her answer.

"Oh...so, I heard," responds Angela, running her tongue over her lips. "But shit! From what I was told, almost all of Duval can say the same about ya homegirl over there." Angela smiles, seeing the look on Devan and Consuela's faces, deciding to run the blade deeper. "Oh... Little Miss Pocahontas ain't tell you she was a hoe before she became a schoolgirl! Don't get me wrong, a high-paid hoe, but a hoe nonetheless!"

Consuela's face turns beet red as she looks around the room, at the many faces, looking at her accusation written on their faces. Judging one of the truths of her life without any knowledge of the reasons she was doing what she was doing. Once Angela sees she's accomplished what she set out to do and Consuela starts to pack her stuff, she tries to say something more, but it is cut short by Devan.

"Well, Angela... If what you say is true, that's the past and nobody knows the reasons for it and you of all people should know that... Just last week at Ben's party, how many niggas did you suck and fuck for free? What Ben, Tony, Antwon, Sam... and about three other niggas, right?" said Devon, locking a flaming mad Angela in the eyes.

"Yeah... Ain't that a bitch! A poor hoe calling a high-paid hoe a hoe! If that ain't the pot calling the kettle black... Come on Consuela. Let's go get lunch."

Consuela timidly stands up, slowly following behind Devon, as Angela stares daggers into her back. Outside in the hallway, Devon spins around, pinning Consuela against the wall. The sudden movement caused her to exhale swiftly.

"Is what Angie said true?" Devon looks her in the eyes, face inches from hers.

In an attempt to return his stare, she just nods her head. "Well, what I said was true too... I don't care about your past... I want you... and just as a warning..." he pauses, lightly running his lips across Consuela's neck, kissing her beating pulse.

As his lips and tongue touch her neck, she feels that familiar feeling of wetness between her legs, yet this is the first time a sense of tightness has entered her chest, her legs feel like string and the only thing holding her up is Devon's body against hers.

When his kisses make their way to her wanting lips, she swallows her anticipation only to be left hanging as he finishes his words. "I will have you... I'm not the shy, timid guy I come off to be when I come for something I want... In this case, must-have." He states, bringing Consuela off that cliff with a long deep kiss, then turning around leaving her to catch her balance as she almost falls.

Leaning against the wall, watching Devon walk away, Consuela attempts to calm the wild beating of her heart, on wobbly knees, standing completely up. Devon is no longer in sight, having turned the corner, leaving her with the thoughts of his win in one of the many battles, that consummate the war for her heart. For Consuela class is over. She has to run home, change pants, after taking a show to wash all of the juice that had run down her legs.

***

"You know..." says Akema hours later looking into a blindfold. "...I have got to stop hanging around you! This is the second time in less than a month I've been drugged and kidnapped by people I don't even fucking know!" "Well" answers Tivia, "You've always said your life was lacking adventures, so... tah-dah!"

"Very funny! But on the real, why are these people after Jizzle?"

"The truth is... Hold up. How did you know my boss' nickname?"

"Now is not the time... to be honest, I know a lot about your boss man, some things only he can tell you, but we'll get to that later. First, we've got to figure a way out of this bullshit we're in now."

"Yeah." sighs Tivia, still pondering Akema's last words. After coming to the realization she isn't going to find out right now, Tivia starts trying to ponder the way out of this situation, when the sound of a door opening, and a light switch flicking stops all of her thoughts.

"Take the blindfolds off," commands a feminine voice. Once they come off, Tivia and Akema's eyes try to focus on the brightness of the room. They finally get to see the slender Japanese woman, about 4'5" standing in front of them, with her hands on her hips.

Tivia finds the command kind of sexy, with her long black hair that falls right over her shoulder, not to mention, the sharp slant of her eyes the Japanese are known for. Yet what catches her attention the most is the swirl of red and black dragons that cover the woman's body, intertwining in some form of a violate embrace, causing blood to flow from their scales.

"Umm... Would you mind telling me why the fuck you drugged us?" exclaims Tivia.

"That was my sister... My name is Chi, but you can call me Venom." Chi said, with a voice that is soft, yet demanding at the same time.

"Umm... No. I'm good, Chi is fine with me. Venom sounds like some kind of comeback character, but back to question one. Why are we here again?"

"That's an easy answer," states Chi, walking towards them with a step that puts Akema in the mind of a martial artist. "A friend or lover of yours took something dear from my brother, and actually sent a videotape of the whole process. The next morning, my brother was missing a rather large sum of money..." She pauses, trying to find the best way to put her next words, "Granted, his wife is lost, I feel was much needed... Yet being he feels otherwise, somebody has to pay for her death." She said, pulling out a photo, "Do you know this man, a Mr. Neiros Simmons?"

Tivia and Akema look at the picture, of a dark-skinned man walking into what looks like the doors of a hotel and burst into a fit of laughter. Chi turns her head slightly to the side, clearly not finding any humor in the situation, and calmly asks, "What...

Is... So... Funny?"

"Hold on. Wait." Tivia tries to gain her composure. "Who told you that was Neiros?"

"This," Chi states, pressing play, showing them the death of Shi'ama. "Damn," exclaims Tivia. "That's fucked up, but that is not a picture of Neiros Simmons."

"Then who is it?" asks Chi, the door slamming open, exposing a medium-built white man who immediately shoots Chi in the body, "Ahhh! Ms. Tivia and Akema... My name is Tavis... Tavis Teams." He says looking down at Chi, "These people were free workers for a smart employer. Ladies, you're coming with me." he finishes, raising a dark gun from behind his back.

"Whoa! Whoa!" screams Akema, getting a pause out of Tavis. "Are the darts necessary?" "Umm...yeah." Pfft, pfft. "Damn Tivia! This is that bull."

Chapter 16

On the flight home, I sit next to my wife, thinking about my life. One thing these past series of events have allowed me to realize, that we as humans always feel we have a total grip on reality. That our lies, we feel are necessary for the concealment of a truth that may hurt others, we see them as foolproof. That we control the things that occur around us, yet we can still come to find that by building a false reality, to be our reality, we in turn are living in the false realities of others. You know this is just like one of them Eureka! moments you have as a kid. To explain this point, I'm not going to use my life as an example. Take the average nigga in the streets selling dope. His reality is more than likely going to be money, cars, and women, which in all essence is a false reality. How? This is how, reality is the hundreds of lives he's destroyed including his own, not to mention his mothers, who more than likely prays for him, only to actually wait for the phone to ring on that one day she'll find out she's outlived him or may have a difficult time seeing him for a long time.

Now, this same hustler will tell you that the last thing he wants is for his son to grow up and be a hustler. How is that? When on a day-to-day basis, all he shows him are the things gained from his life. Never taking the time to sit him down and explain to him the downsides. Because truth be told, he doesn't have the time. That's how the streets strive, they build up a plethora of fake concerns that take you away from the reality that matters.

I hope at least one of the "real" niggas reading this shit takes that to heart. I mean look at me. I was one hundred percent positive all my realities were on point. Truth of the matter. In reality, I was a deadbeat dad, a whoremonger. Shit, my wife's been an assassin for years, and me as an assassin, never even saw it! Now I question you, my nigga. How many realities have your false realities made you miss out on?

"You're not going to sleep?" asks Sienna, sitting next to me, and for the first time in all of our time together, I finally see why I don't have the love for her that I should. The reason is most of us men just look at women purely on a physical level.

Which gives us that, it's about my shawty, fuck my baby mama type of attitude, yet without this beautiful woman sitting next to me, my little girl wouldn't be possible. The question now is, being that I've finally seen Sienna for the first time: Am I ready to be that man for her? Time will tell.

"Now Si... I'm just thinking about all the bullshit we've got before us once we hit the Ville."

"No kidding." She stretches, yawning, looking sexy as fuck. "What's the play?"

"Huh?"

"I'm following your lead on this one."

"What?"

"Yeah, I've been thinking myself, sometimes, it's not just the person you sleep next to that has to change, but you as well."

"So, the whole me out to kill you and vice versa?"

"On the back burner. Indefinitely...for now."

"For now?"

"Yeah." She looks me in the eyes. "This way, if it doesn't work., at least I can say I tried my hardest."

"Oh yeah... That's what it do, but um, speaking of hard..." I said, playing with Sienna's silky curls.

"Boy! No!" She responds, slapping my hand away. "We are on a plane!"

"And? You ain't got to use the bathroom."

"You see, that's your problem! Here it is, we're about to have to take on two assassins, and all you can think about is sex." "Bae, I told you... I'm fucked up." I shrug, smiling. "Yeah, you are, but..." She says, looking around at the rest of the passengers, "...so am I when it comes to yo crazy ass. Come to the bathroom in two minutes!" she dashes around me, strutting up the aisle, being sure to put a little something extra in the walk. Damn! Who would think this sexy muthafucka is a damn killer? But shit, it doesn't matter now, I'm about to go kill that pussy!

Almost an hour or two later, I and Si walk through J.I.A., being sure to keep all of our senses on one hundred, yet in my opinion, nobody is going to be brave enough to attack us this soon. That would be an amateur mistake.

You see, at this point, it's only common sense that we would be alert, and just as both me and Sienna have access to airport-proof pistols. Which we're both concealing in a specially made case designed to look like the average book under an x-ray machine.

I'm pretty sure other assassins know about and have access to the same type of hardware. Plus, the assassin game ain't really played like the movies depict it to be played. Well, almost, but not all the way. For instance, in the movies, the hit would've taken place at the airport. So the would-be assassins fade into the crowd, but let's look at that in reality. As I walk through J.I.A., the main thing I notice is cameras everywhere, not to mention security. The whole fade into the crowd situation would be damn near impossible under these circumstances. Then there's the 911 factor. These muthafuckas have been on alert for any suspicious behavior. So it's a safe assumption to say nobody is going to be stupid enough to draw attention to us or them.

"Neiros," Sienna says, bringing me out of my thoughts.

"What's up bae?"

"Could you go to Cinnabon and get me something while I freshen up?"

"No problem... What do you want?"

"Surprise me." She smiles over her shoulder, heading towards the women's room.

Watching her walk away, I call Tivia's cellphone for the third time only to get her answering machine, which has me kind of worried. It's not often that Tivia doesn't answer her cell, and even if she's busy, she'd at least text me to let me know.

"What is it Jizzle?" Murder says.

"Shit... But aye, you seen Tivia around anywhere?"

"To be honest...naw. What's up?"

"She ain't answering her phone and we need to find a place to record, plus find out who burnt down the studio in the first place."

"I'm on that... Also, I've set up two more spots as well." Murder said, talking about two more traps. Oh, I forget to tell y'all, once Gut One got flipped, I put Murder in charge of the dope business. Shit, to be honest, so far he's been holding shit down, but I got to get up with him on the one on one, and put it all on the table.

"That's what it do," I reply. "Get at me later. Me and wifey got to get some sleep, jet lag, and shit. I'm about to go home and crash."

"That's what it do." Murder said, hanging the phone up, looking at his next in command. A childhood friend by the name of Block.

Just one look at the 5'11" male and you'll understand how he got his name. Everything from his square-shaped head and square frame gave him the appearance of being a human cinder block.

Murder and Block met at the age of six on the way to elementary school. Murder, being one of the only white boys to attend Springfield Elementary, caught as much hell as anyone at that age could hope not to find, but even then, he knew he had to show the hood he was tougher than everyone. On one hot summer day, just before the beginning of the summer break, the sun was tanning his neck a deep shade of red. Murder was surrounded by some of the neighborhood bullies when Block came to his rescue. Granted, they both got beat up together. They've been down for each other on everything from petty theft to murder.

"Yo Murder nigga... What is Jizzle talking about?"

"He bought to go catch some rest and shit... Did you find out what's the deal with dem niggas in Ft. Caroline?" asked Murder, referring to a small group of niggas that don't want to get with his get down or lay down plan.

One of the biggest obstacles Murder has faced his entire life, is his skin color. Most blacks in the streets don't live in a reality where a white boy has the power and heart to take over. To them, there ain't no way in the hell or high water a white boy trying to be black has got the balls to take some shit over, but if they only knew their point of view is their greatest weakness because it's impossible to act a color. Everybody regardless of their race or color can be raised to be that nigga in the streets.

"Actually my nigga." Block responds, "I think the only way dem nigga are going to see real shit is if we show em."

"Hmm."

"Yeah, the other day, about three of dem niggas tried to kick in the door, but Neek dem niggas stopped em in time." "In time! Nigga they should've shot dem flaw ass niggas through the door as soon as they raise their foot! What the fuck we got cameras for?" Murder exclaims.

211

"Yeah... That's some other shit to run by you... Neek and his niggas was into some pussy... So they weren't on point."

"Hmmf." Breathes Murder, taking a sip of his bottle of gin. One of the things he hoped wouldn't happen, was that his crew would allow the same thing that happens to these street cats, to happen to them.

Snatching the thought out of his head, Block says, "Listen Murder, even though you got a couple of bodies under your belt, all these niggas still believe you ain't living like that. And just being honest, the streets screaming all those bodies was just a fluke...you ain't really mean to merc shit...so everybody still thinks—"

"Shit pussy." Murder spits with an all too familiar look in his eyes, one Block loves to see, because that means shit is about to get ugly.

Block doesn't know if Murder knows it or not, but in some ways, he admires him. Block has seen this white boy go through everything from his mother being a crackhead, tricking with every man in the neighborhood, to his father beating his ass for his own guilt of being a failure. Yet Murder, whose real name is Robbie, has overcome all of the hardships life has thrown at him. For that alone, Block has more respect for him than he has for any other man on Earth, with the exception of his own father.

"So," He says, passing Murder the blunt in his hand, "What's up?"

"Do you really have to ask?"

"When do we slide?"

"Shit... Now's a better time than any."

Forty-five minutes later, they pull up, parking in front of one of the traps he has in this area. Neek, a medium-height red nigga, comes outside followed by two females and one of his workers.

212

Looking at Neek bounce down the stairs like nothing is wrong, Murder tells himself he's not even mad for what is about to happen.

"Murder! Shit, my nigga! What it do?" Neek embraces Murder.

"Shit...Block told me some niggas tried to kick ya door in the other day. You handled dat?"

"Naw...I got some niggas on it, but they ain't get shit. It ain't really that serious. Know what I'm saying?"

"Hmm...not that serious, huh?" Murder smirks. "You know who it was?"

"Yeah, even know where they live."

"Yeah! Where?"

"Over in the Plaza. Apartment 137, if I'm correct."

"They trappin?"

"Yeah."

"Oh, so you layin on em till they about to re-up?"

"Why do that?" Neek answers perplexed, "Brah, we got it over here! Damn dem niggas!"

"Yeah." Murder states, and before Neek can brace himself, he whips out his pistol, shooting him in the leg. The two women with him scream loud enough to wake the dead as Neek's worker puts both his hands up, clearly not wanting anything to do with the situation.

"Yo!" He yells when Block draws down on him, "Aye! I told that nigga he was tripping! But I'm just a foot soulja!"

"I feel dat." Murder calmly says, "Gone and get these bitches out of here, and I'll holla at you in a minute."

"Alright." The young soulja says, quickly pulling both the women into the apartment.

"Listen," Murder says, with a voice full of venom, kneeling down to allow Neek to hear him clearly. "Do you understand why this is happening? I don't think you do. So, this is why I feel like you think this shit is sweet, but brah...it ain't."

"Listen Murder, listen, it ain't like dat. I just ain't see dem niggas bringing no pressure like that brah." Says Neek, clutching his leg.

"Hmmf. Listen Neek, it ain't just about dem petty ass, wannabe hustlers. It's more than that. The thing is if you don't see it, den you ain't supposed to." "Brah, brah...listen...listen!" He pleads.

"You damn sho want me to do a lot of that."

"Come on brah, I know I was getting too relaxed, but spare a nigga brah!"

"Oh, I am sparing you brah, on the strength of yo momma alone, even though I don't know her. Yet I'm sure she doesn't want her son to die before she does, but the thing is... I'll only deal with the momma card once. Next time I'll just send her enough cash to send you off real nice, plus enough to live good for a while, ya feel me?" He slaps Neek on his leg.

"Yeah, yeah brah. I feel ya." Neek grimaces from the pain.

"Yo Block!"

"What's up Merc?"

"Do me a favor brah and take this nigga to Memorial... I'm a go holla at brah in the trap."

"No problem." Block helps Neek up, putting him in the car. Once they pull off, Murder walks into the apartment, to find the young soulja trying to calm the women down. "Listen." He says, "Y'all can't be acting all scared and shit! A nigga would hate to take y'all as a threat, ya know."

"Naw, naw, a threat? Never that." Murder walks through the door, both women immediately tensing upon his entrance, which he actually finds sort of funny. For he knows that before the incident, they probably swore that Neek was really living like that. Not saying he isn't, but he just ain't on the level Murder is. "What y'all's name shawty?" He asks, with one of his friendly white boy smiles.

"Sh, Shawanna." says a petite, caramel-complexioned girl, with a short Amber Rose cut. Looking at her size A breast, Murder kind of thinks she's okay. Then, once he looks at her face. He realizes she would be of average looks, if not for the tears running down her face.

"And yours?" He turns to her friend, who from the first look, he knows must be Neek's shawty, because the girl is bad! Murder can't help but compliment Neek's taste, as he stares into her amber-colored eyes, which have a cat-like feel to them. Everything from her firm breast to her flawless skin spelled perfection. Due to the fact that she's standing up, Murder gets the chance to admire her small waist, and what looks like a 34, 26, 45 frame.

"Who? Me? Oh, my name is Tiffani." She answers, with a head motion causing her honey-brown hair to shimmer.

"You don't look as distraught as your friend here." Murder says.

"Oh Shawn, that's because she ain't hood like that," responds Tiffani with just enough swag to not be too ghetto.

"Oh, and I guess you are?"

"Boy, I was raised around guns."

"...but you screamed too."

"That was because I was more shocked than anything. I mean,

I ain't see that shit coming."

"Why? Because I'm a white boy?"

"Yeah, that too, but mainly because you was too cool."

"That's real." Murder smiles, really feeling Tiffani. Most women would've left the whole that too comment out, and just went with the too cool response. He honesty gave her a plus in his book. "But peep this." He continues. "How about I compensate y'all for your time. Lil brah, drop about five stacks on em. Tiffani, I would like to keep in contact with you.

How long you known my niggas?"

"About two or three days, and before you think it, I ain't some freak hoe fucking one thousand. Ya nigga wasn't getting none tonight!" She crosses her arms across her chest, which Murder finds cute.

"Who said I thought that?" he smirks.

"You a dope boy." She rolls her head. "All y'all think that."

"Well, I ain't just a dope boy... I'm a rapper too."

"Oooh! Oh shit!" Shawanna screams, causing everybody to jump including Tiffani. "I knew it! I knew I knew yo face! You Murder! With Jizzle's label!"

"Yeah." Murder beams at the recognition but instantly notices Tiffani still has an unimpressed look on her face. "You gone let me get at you, Tiffani?"

"No, and you can keep ya money!" She snaps, a lot colder than Murder was ready for. "Shawn! Let's go!" "But Tiff!" Pouts Shawanna.

"Now!" She screams, making Shawanna jump, starting to gather her things.

Murder watches as the women hurry to gather their belongings, wonder what is the matter, yet before he can investigate the situation, the door slams, leaving him and his companion standing in utter silence.

*** "Yeah, I'm about to meet up with him now. Yeah. Yeah. I'll be home soon; I understand the weather is bad... Love you too. One." Block said, hanging up the phone on a stormy night in August. He knows he shouldn't be out in this tropical storm, but money waits on no man. So here he is waiting for his connect with fifty thousand dollars worth of drug money in the car and his companion.

"Damn! This muthafuckin storm ain't playing!" Murder said, getting in the car wet, slamming the door.

"Murder, nigga what's up?" Block daps him up.

216

"You know, getting this money. You mind if a nigga chill for a minute while the storm calms down?"

"Naw brah. We good and ducked off." Block referred to their location, a dead-end off of Hogan Road.

The area is the perfect place to conduct business, being as secluded as it is, tonight even more with the storm out. The four residents on the road aren't even thinking about looking out the window.

"What's been good wit chu?" inquires Murder, puffing on a blunt Block passed him.

"Truthfully, everything my nigga! Business been locking up, and with this blessing for these fifty you bout to shoot me, ain't no looking back!"

"Yeah. That's what it do. The fam good?" Murder said, looking out at the storm as it subsides a little.

"Yeah, yeah, as a matter of fact, here go my people now."

Block said, answering his cellphone, "Yo... Yeah, I'm with my nigga Murder now. Yeah, yeah...I told you I'll be home—" Boo! Boo! Murder cuts Block's sentence short with shots to the head. Shaking his head, he listens as the voice on the other end of the phone screams the man's name, in hopes of an answer.

To the eye, this situation is going to look like a robbery gone wrong, but really the situation is bigger than that. Two weeks ago, Block sent two of his goons to one of Murder's spots.

The thing is, he didn't know that Murder was the connect to the spot. So once Murder found out, he called Block and offered him a deal he couldn't refuse, the brick of cane for fifty stacks. Of course, greed got in the way of logic. Thus, his death today.

Picking Block's phone up, he says "Listen, whoever this nigga is to you, he's nobody now. In life, everything becomes 360. Only the ones prepared for the come around can survive." He tosses the phone down, pulling out some

217

gasoline from his duffle bag, setting the car and all evidence on fire. ***

Tiffani sits in her car remembering the night Murder told her that he killed her brother, the last family member she had on Earth.

Then, she couldn't put a face to the name, but now she has. "Damn!" She slams her fists against the steering wheel, causing Shawn to jump in the seat next to her. The attack on the steering wheel isn't a wave of anger, but frustration. For out of anger, she moved too quickly, but she smiles to herself. She can fix her mistake. Because Murder wants her body, but what he doesn't know is, this pussy is going to be a killer.

***

Murder looks out the blinds, somewhat baffled by Tiffani's sudden want to leave. Thinking to himself to make it his business to find out her reasons. Still looking out the window, he says, "Yo... What's ya name Git?"

"Who? Me?"

"Naw...the other muthafucka in the room!" Murder looks at the young man, a look of frustration on his face.

"Oh, my bad. Young."

"Young, listen, you know where them niggas that tried to pull the kick door live at?"

"Yeah, over in the plaza."

"You know the apartment?"

"Yep. Apartment 137. Why? What's up?" Young said, and Murder can see the impatience to prove his worth in the young man's eyes.

"Strap up." Is all he says, walking out the door, Young eagerly following behind him.

Driving out of Ft. Coraline Arms, the Plaza Apartments aren't even a good block away, but Murder, having committed crimes of this nature plenty of times, easily concocts a plan before they arrive.

At the entrance of the apartments, he drops Young off, being sure to drive slower than usual to arrive at his destination. Parking the car, he checks his pistol, tucking it in his waist, then strolling up to apartment 137 knocking on the door.

"Yeah!" comes a deep voice from behind the door.

"Y'all good?"

"Yeah, yeah." The door opens, revealing a slightly built red-skinned male. "What you trying to cop?"

"Shit...a nine if you got it." Murder responds, to see where the dude's mind is. For there is no way he would serve anybody a nine-piece without knowing.

"A nine?" The man answers, "How you know to even come at

me like that..."

"My nigga upfront told me y'all got it." murder answers, putting his hands up defensively.

"Oh yeah." The man smiles, "Oh...come in."

Murder walks in the door baffled and upset at the same time. Baffled that without knowing him, these dudes would sell him nine ounces, on the strength of some unknown nigga upfront. Upset because Neek even allowed some absent-minded niggas like this to even attempt to rob him!

"Damn homie." The man said, "You look real familiar." He said, looking Murder in the face.

"Yeah...I'm a rapper."

"Rapper."

"Yeah...Murder. Signed to Fake Reality Records."

"Oh shit!" The man yells, astonished. "Damn homie. We got all yo mixtapes up in this bitch!"

"Yeah... That's what it do."

"But damn... Why are you over here trying to cop from us?" The moment he finishes that question, as if that was his cue,

219

Young let the A.K. 47 he has with him sing like Whitney Houston. The sudden burst of gunfire catches the man and his two accomplices off guard, giving Murder the moment he needs to pull out his pistol, firing at will.

Backing up towards the door, the assault is more like a slaughter. As Young's assault rifle unleashes a string of death from the side window while Murder's .45 aids it.

Once the deed is done, Murder quickly exits the apartment, meeting Young at his car that is already running. The duo quickly makes a swift getaway. The whole time Young realizes he may have just found his next boss.

Chapter 17

Neo sits in Kane's living room after a hit they decided to undertake together. Yeah, the payout with Neiros was enough to really sit them right for a long time, but one thing about greed is, it's never ceases to be hungry. There is a saying that goes; The only thing that can fill the appetite of man is the grave.

Meaning that a greedy man will not cease to be satisfied until he dies. Neo and Kane are prime examples of such greed. Despite the million-dollar payoff, the duo still decided to take a job for fifty thousand dollars, only receiving twenty-five thousand a piece.

Sitting on the sofa thinking about it, Neo also realizes that it really isn't about the cash for them. The actual thrill of the kill means more than anything. Some people were put on this Earth to be good doctors, lawyers, police, etc. and they really excel at said occupations. For Neo and Kane, they were placed on this planet to be the ultimate predators. The thrill of stalking, subduing, and slaughtering their prey, is ten times more rewarding than any amount of money they could be paid.

"Kane!" yells Neo, "Goddamn! How long does it take to grab something to fucking drink!" He exclaims, "Kane…Kane?"

Getting no response, he decides to go look for his counterpart that has become more of a brother to him. They both met each other at the young age of fifteen and immediately realized that they both had a natural talent for murder.

After only six months of knowing each other, they committed their first murder together on a local bully that picked the wrong geek to pick on, Kane's younger brother. Once they completed their first murder together, from that moment on, their only goal was to perfect an art they both enjoyed conducting.

Walking into the kitchen, Neo finds Kane seated at the kitchen table with his head down. "Damn brother. You decided to get drunk without me, you bastard!" He taps him on the shoulder. "Kane!" He taps him again, he doesn't move, "Man wake up!" He pushes him out of frustration, backing up when Kane falls over-exposing his slit throat, blood pooling under him.

"What the fuck!" Neo exclaims.

"It's totally different when you're the prey, huh?" a voice said from behind him, causing him to turn around.

"What?" Neo said, flabbergasted, looking at the athletic-built Hispanic male dressed in a nice, expensive suit.

"The feeling...it's different when you're the prey."

"Listen muthafucka...I don't know who you are, but I do know what you're about to be...Dead!"

"Really?" The man raises his eyebrows, chuckling slightly.

"You think this shit is funny?" Neo says, pulling a knife off the counter, throwing it at the man, only to be shocked when he dodges it without even taking his hands out of his pockets. Out of sheer frustration, Neo rushes the man, attempting to push him with a combination of strikes, ranging from straight jabs to overhands, only to be easily weaved, parried, and slipped.

The man moves out of the way as Neo picks the medium-sized kitchen table up, tossing it at him. The crash as it slams against the glass pane door is deafening. "Is that all you've got?" The man smiles.

"Only getting started!" Kane breathes, engaging the man with a series of kicks and punches, landing only two strikes. The last being a solid right cross to the mouth.

"Now... We're getting somewhere." The man backs up. "My turn." He said, swiftly approaching Neo with a feint, causing

222

him to throw a straight jab, which he counters with a paksao, reversing Neo's strike hitting him with a back fist straight to the stomach. Immediately continuing his momentum, spinning on his front leg, rising to attack Neo with a spinning axe kick to the right shoulder.

The attack is almost crippling as Neo catches himself with a firm hand on the ground, just barely escaping a spinning kick to the side of the head.

Backing up, panting heavily, Neo's anger rises at the sight of the man standing calmly in front of him without the slightest sign of fatigue.

"One more time... For it all." The man smirks, stepping toward Neo. Once in range, Neo attempts to beat him to the punch. Throwing a jab, spinning with an elbow, both of which the man easily blocks, countering the attacks with an uppercut to the armpit, overhand elbows to the temple, and in one of the swiftest motions he's ever seen, the man spins, sweeping him, in the same motion, pulling out a .9mm.

Neo grimaces as the checkmate move gives him just enough time to see the flash from the bullet exiting the barrel, bringing the same fate he's dealt with so many...Death. The bullet enters his throat as another enters his chest.

The smile on the man's face is extremely more painful than the end he's dealt him.

"Truthfully." he sighs as Neo's life seeps out of his body. "I really thought the two of you would be a challenge...guess I was wrong. Let's hope the rest are."

The hole in his throat eliminates any chance he has to respond.

So as the last of his life's light extinguishes, the only thought he has in his mind is...he hopes Hamzah's ready.

Flow walks up Lefferts Blvd a couple of weeks later, after his conversation with Damone. Which ended with Damone giving him ten kilos of heroin to push up north in his home city of New York.

Walking towards the train station on Lefforts and Liberty Ave, he reminisces about the reason he had to clear it in the first place...

"Flow, don't you think it's time we stop playing all these games?" Said Nikki, a Puerto Rican beauty, about 4'8" with thick thighs like Rihanna, but two times the ass. Flow stares into her coffee-brown eyes, her curly locks blowing in the slight breeze given on this stuffy July night.

"What game Ma?" He answers.

"This whole boyfriend-girlfriend shit we got going on!" replies Nikki.

"What? You trying to propose to me or some shit?" states Flow, watching two dudes across the street eyeing him from the Hot-N-Spicy.

As the men start towards 123rd away from Liberty, Flow notices they continue to keep their eyes trained on him. With a nonchalant move, he spins around, while embracing Nikki at the same time, noticing another due walking up Liberty towards him. Immediately he puts two and two together.

"Are you even listening to me!" exclaims Nikki with a forceful slap on his chest.

"Yeah..." Flow casually lets Nikki go, easing his hand under his shirt, taking the safety off his Heckler and Koch nine-millimeter. "I hear ya Ma! But I ain't gone sit up here and tell you settling down is in my immediate future plans." he finishes, just as he notices the first two coming back up 123rd towards him.

"Why? Is it somebody else!" cries Nikki, tears falling down her angelic face, reminding Flow of the one aspect about Nikki he hates, she's an emotional rollercoaster!

"Nikki...peep this, I'm a need you to leave."

"No! No! I'm not going anywhere!" states Nikki, fire in her eyes.

"Listen, now ain't the time for this!" Flow says as calmly as he possibly can, as not to alert his pursuers that he's onto them. As bad as he wants, he knows now is not a time to lose his cool, but Nikki is pushing his patience to the limit.

"Listen boy, you are going to answer me today!" She tells him, just as one of the four men goes under his shirt, pulling out a pistol.

On instinct alone, Flow pulls his gun, pushing Nikki to the ground, sending three shots towards Liberty Blvd.

The first duo also returns fire, while retreating to do so, to allow the two men on 123rd to close in on Flow. Not noticing the move, Flow starts to pursue the shooter, only to catch a bullet to the shoulders, sending him flying forward. Yet being the soldier he is, he goes with the momentum, falling on his back, catching his attackers off guard as he puts four bullets into motion. Three of them hit their intended mark.

"Fuck!" he screams, standing up, feeling the pain from the gunshot wound spike through his body. "Nikki." He calls out, walking up to the motionless form lying face-first on the concrete. "Yo! Nikki! We gotta go!" He states, turning her over only to find the left side of her head missing, a dead stare in her eyes. "Damn!" Flow said to himself, granted he didn't love Nikki, he definitely didn't want to see her like this.

Knowing Nikki is beyond any form of assistance. Flow quickly hops in his Dodge Durango, making his way towards his home in East New York, Brooklyn.

Packing his stash of drugs and money, kneeling down to put the combination into his safe, he stops when his cellphone starts playing "99 Problems" by Jay-z, a clear indication an unknown number is calling. "State yo claim."

"I almost claimed ya life, son." an unfamiliar voice states.

"Well, son! Almost doesn't count in my book." answers Flow,

"But who wants to claim it?"

"Now now... I'll see about ya when you return."

"How do you know I'm leaving?"

"Because that's the move I'd make." The voice answers, before hanging up.

***

"Amor de Rey!" Someone said, bringing Flow back to the present.

Looking around, he finds Smash. A sixteen-year-old Dominican youth, with the heart of a lion and the patience of a bull. To say that Flow and Smash are look-alikes would be an understatement.

Flow looks at the 5'10" young Dominican, seeing himself at that age, just like him. Smash is a pretty boy type, all the way to his long hair and boyish looks. Yet just like Flow, Smash is all about his issues. Most of his foes underestimate him, falling victim to his guns when his temper goes out the window.

"Amor de Rey!" Flow returns, greeting Smash with the common one used in the Latin King Nation they've both been members of since birth.

"Long time no see." Smash looks Flow in the eyes with an expression that only a killer would recognize. Void of sympathy. It can only be acquired through experiencing tragic moments. And for Smash, that's been the case since the age of ten, being forced to watch his father get gunned down in the streets.

"Yeah, I had to get out of sight for a minute. Where you headed?"

"Me? Bout to catch the A-train to east New York. You?" Smash questions, passing Flow a cush-filled Garcia Vega.

226

"Shit." Flow inhales the potent smoke. "Bout to head the same way."

"That's what it is."

Finishing the blunt just in time to catch the A-train, the two settle down in the back of one of the carts. Flow looks around and starts to realize how much he's missed his city. Just looking around at all the people getting on the train makes him wonder how people down south survive in the antisocial attitude bred by their society.

In Florida, Flow had to go out of his way to meet people.

Versus here, people spend more time in the streets on foot.

"What's been good with you?" Flow asked Smash.

"Just got out on a three-year bid about a month ago."

"How about Rel?" Flow inquiries about his older brother.

"He's doing his thing and all."

"Well." Flow starts, realizing admiring how the young man gives his only short answers, not knowing where this line of questioning is going. "I'm going to start up a company."

"Who are you hiring?"

"Right now I only got ten men on my payroll."

"Really? Ten men."

"Yeah. I need a partner to invest with, but he gotta be ready to start a hostile takeover."

"Mm...hmm."

"Yeah, I plan on buying a lot of shares in another company real soon."

"That sounds good, but you've been M.I.A. for a minute, and I know about ya reason for leaving."

"Uh. Huh." Flow nods, knowing where this is going.

"Now you pop up wanting to start a company? Not to mention one of such size. I must question, who do you have backing you?"

"I totally understand." Flow smiles, impressed by Smash's outlook. "When I left, I went down south, hooked up with the C.E.O. of a monopoly. You know, put in some work, did my thang and the almighty blessed me. You of all people should know. I've never been one to trade secrets on the stock market."

"Word. Word." Smash acknowledges his point because he knows about a lot of things Flow's done with his brother Rel and how many times they've been down in front of the police, neither of them saying a word. "So, what do you want from me?"

"I need a president and vice president... You got anybody in mind?"

"Yeah. Of course myself, and then my cousin Junior."

"How many shares can I invest in your franchise?"

"Bout one or two to start," Smash replied. Flow can see the hustler in his eyes. For Smash, this is an opportunity he can't afford to let pass and isn't going to.

"Alright. We can do that," said Flow.

After exchanging numbers, the two part ways with plans to meet the next day. Flow walks through East New York feeling at home with each step. Because unlike down south, people are sitting on their front porches, instead of hiding inside their homes.

Just the sight of the homes sitting so close together made Flow miss being home even more. "So... You finally decided to show back up? Huh, Papi?" an angelic voice says, too familiar to his ears.

Looking to his right, he finds the first and possibly the only love in his life, Ni'ancy, a Portuguese/Puerto Rican beauty with natural green eyes. The color of the darkest emeralds.

Flow's heart stops as his eyes take her in. Then his own eyes start to travel from hers to her subtle lips while admiring her nicely shaded caramel skin. "What... You just gone stand there, staring or can I get a hug!" She walks across 76th street, forcing her hips to sway in motion that is borderline hypnotic, stirring up something deep inside of Flow he'd forgotten existed.

"You can get a lot more than a hug Mami." Flow states, scooping Ni'ancy up into his arms, smiling to himself as she lets out one of those girlish giggles he's missed so much. "Ohh!" he says, once he places her on the ground and she punches him in the chest. "What was that for?"

"That was for leaving me!" She states with a pout.

"Listen Ma... I ain't really have time to stop and smell the roses if you peep what I'm saying."

"No! I don't! You could've taken me with you!"

"You saying you would've dropped everything and just left with me Ma? Come on now!" Flow said, cocking his head to the side.

"Believe it or not yes, I would've," answers Ni'ancy, looking Flow in the eyes.

Flow stands in front of her and he can tell she's being truthful. It's all in her eyes, and as much as he doesn't want to admit it, he knew the day he left, she would've gone with him, but he couldn't allow her to fuck her life up as well.

"So," he said, to break the awkward silence between them. "What's been good with ya? You tied to anybody right now?"

"After you left, I finished school and started attending Queens College... I'm in my last year."

"That's real. What are you majoring in?"

"Business Management. I want to start a couple of businesses once I'm done."

"Hmm." Remarks Flow, "You still haven't answered my other question."

"Am I tied to anybody? Yeah, his name is Amari." She smiles.

"You into this dude?" Flow asks, totally deflated.

"More than I've ever been into anybody in my entire life!"

229

"Damn!" Remarks Flow, taking a blow into his ego. "How old is this dude?"

"Amari? He turns four this year."

"Four! Oh shit! You got a shorty? Who's the baby daddy?" He asks but gets cut off before she can answer.

"Amor de Rey!" He hears from behind him.

Turning to see his childhood friend, he explodes, "Oh shit! Amor de Rey!" He greets, embracing Rez, his brother through trials. Even though Rez is a year older than him, they've been tight since their younger days. When the only number that mattered to them was the number of bills in their pockets.

"Yo Ni'ancy I gotta get going with you later. Me and my brother got some catching up to do." Flow said, not even giving Ni'ancy time to respond. As the two men walk off, Flow is oblivious of the hurt look that is plastered on her face.

"Bro, It's bout time you come home!" Rez said, "I mean you left me that short ass message and shit, then disappeared!"

"My bad bro, shit was crazy as fuck, but what's been good with you?" Flow watches Rez as he splits a Dutch.

"Same ole sht... You know trying to fill a King's plate."

"Is it full?"

"Bro, you know a King's pate is never full, but besides the normal operation, I've taken Atlantic Blvd from that clown Carmelo."

"Word! How much?"

"All his shit from 11th to 116th."

"What you pushing?"

"Both the kids."

"Well, that's good. I got a couple of boys I need to orphan. Ya feel me?"

"How many?"

230

"Bout eight sons." Flow said, being sure to talk in code. Because one thing about New York, you never know who's listening, and some conversations are easy to get around in court. "You think you can find a shelter for them?"

"Where they come from?"

"Florida."

"Florida! I don't know if they'll be able to adopt up here Flow... I mean, it gets cold son."

"Yeah. I know most of the time you usually get girls from down that way wanting a higher education. But these little dudes, they on point. Their father was a foreigner that met one of my close friends in Duval, but they ain't like it down there. So, I decided to see if New York was a spot they'd like." "Yeah," Rez responds, with a slight head nod, pulling on the almost gone Dutch. "I'll tell you what, bring em by the house later on tonight and I'll let them play a little bit, introduce em to the fam, see how much they take to the environment, and we'll go from there."

"That's what it is, but I know they use to live around nineteen- to twenty-year-olds, so we'll see."

"Damn! Twenty-year-olds? They acting grown like that?" Responds Rez, acknowledging what kind of cut the heroin can take.

"Yeah, that's who they're used to living around, but they're still acting like little boys."

"That's what's good. You seen Smash yet?' Rez asks about his little brother.

"Yeah. Yeah. Politicked with him on the train right before I came this way."

"Yeah. That's good. Little brah kinda not on speaking terms with me, naw mean?" Rez said, the hurt apparent on his face. "What happened?"

"You know, bullshit. In the midst of me taking Carmelo on, he merced Ma and shit. I think Smash still blames me for that shit."

"Damn son, he must've been up the road while that shit was going down."

"Yeah. I tried to talk to him. Even bodied that clown Carmelo and his fam, but dat lil nigga is out of control. The thing is; his mind is years ahead of his peers. While they're on the same high school shit. Smash is on some business exec, conglomerate type shit."

"Yeah." Flow answers, grinning on the inside. That was the reassurance he needed. Now it's just time to let this shit bubble!

Chapter 18

Sitting on his porch after Asr Salah, Hamzah ponders the news of the previous days. Once he learned about the deaths of Neo and Kane, he was definitely on edge. Granted, the soulless brothers ran in a tighter group than the three of them together. So there is no telling what they could've gotten themselves involved in.

As for himself, becoming a million dollars ricer, he did just as he promised his Lord and put the guns and murder down. So mainly that is what concerns him; the if's. What if someone is targeting all three of them? That would leave him the last person on the list.

What if Consuela is in danger? Allah knows better than he. The last thing he wants for her is more heartache.

Since her arrival, Hamzah would be lying if he said he has been impressed with the progress she's making. It's a real task for a female to come from the background she's come from and complete a 180 degree turn into something totally opposite of her usual.

Most young girls in her position usually run back to the nightmare they've hated so much. Why?... As sad as an answer as it is, it's all they truly know. For them, the nightmare is a reality while a dream is only, and will remain that. A dream. A fairytale told to each other in the late-night full of drug abuse and prostitution.

Who could convince a doctor who's practiced medicine for his entire life to do otherwise? That's their dilemma. Who can tell a little girl, given to prostitution by those she swore would protect her, that what she is doing is wrong and there's a better way? Not many.

"Hamzah!" Consuela yells, bringing him out of his contemplation. "Dinner is ready."

Walking into the dining room, Hamzah's mouth automatically starts to water at the sight of the roasted lamb, early peas, and long grain rice with gravy, on his plate. Sitting down in front of the feast, his stomach growls with anticipation. Blessing the meal by saying Bismillah which means In the name of God, he starts to eat using only his right hand.

One of the ways of the Prophet Muhammad, which is in Islam is called the sunnah, is to eat with the right hand only. Consuming his meal in that fashion, Hamzah glances up at Consuela, who has an expression on her face signifying something on her mind. Being the concerned person he is, he takes a mental note to ask her once the meal is finished, yet that moment may never come as the phone rings, interrupting their meal. "Jizzle...please tell me you've got a lawn service and just so happen to be in need of some help," Hamzah states, looking at the number on the caller I.D., answering the phone.

One thing he can be certain of if Neiros is calling is not to go on a vacation unless somebody has to die.

"You'd actually come help me?" he states.

"I would come run the entire business by myself if it meant not being involved in whatever you're calling about."

"Damn homey, you act like every time I call, somebody gotta die or something!"

"Well..." Hamzah responds, waiting to hear the reason for his call.

"I need ya...somebody gotta die."

"That's not shocking!" Hamzah puts his hand on his forehead.

"Hamzah, listen, I know all about the vow you took. And honestly, if I was going up against anybody besides Hunter... I wouldn't even waste your time. I'll tell you what. Come to my house in San Marco and you can decide for yourself."

"Why?"

"I've got something to show you and I hope you're not squeamish."

*** "You know the one thing I find so amazing about you?" Devon asks later that night, sitting across from Consuela at McDonalds on University Blvd on what's called, Town and Country.

"What is that?" She asks, looking into his eyes for the first time in her life, finally understanding what love can possibly mean. For Consuela, Devan is an enigma. Not only does he treat her like a lady, but he has yet to try and get the one thing all men she's known want... her body.

"I find it amazing," He starts while dipping one of his chicken nuggets in honey mustard sauce. "With all the wealth you have... You still choose to eat at a place like this and shop at

Plato's. Why is that?"

"First," Consuela says, with a slight giggle, amazed by his statement, being she's yet to tell him about the small fortune she has. "Why do you assume I have wealth?" "I've seen Hamzah's house. I also know how much he loves you and would give you anything you want." "So you're saying his wealth is my wealth?"

"Well...yeah. You can't tell me if you told Hamzah you wanted the word, he wouldn't try his hardest to give it to you?"

"You don't know Hamzah that well then. Not saying what you said isn't true, but Hamzah is the main reason I live such a fragile lifestyle. He taught me that the treasures of this world are not the important issues. It's the treasures of the afterlife that matter."

"Sounds to me like you're about to become Muslim or something," Devon said with a curious look on his face.

"To be honest." She casts her eyes down. She knows that her answer isn't the one he will want to hear, but she also feels if he's going to be with her, he must respect her mind. "I've already taken my Shahada."

"Shahada...what's that?" Devon asks, knowing the answer isn't one he's going to want to hear. "It is..." Consuela says with a sense of pride in her voice.

"...Ash-shady Anla Illaha Ill Allah Wa Ash-shady Anna Muhammud-ar-Rasulallah! There is no God except Allah and

Muhammad is His servant and messenger!"

At the declaration of faith, all Muslims must recite this in order to enter the fold of Islam. Devon pauses, staring at Consuela for the next few minutes, the only thought going through his mind, Damn!

"Um...um." He stutters, looking at a confident Consuela. "...but you're not wearing that thingy." he motions with his hand around his head.

"The hijab?" She answers. "No...but that's why I'm wearing this headscarf. If you really look at how I'm dressed, in clothing two times my size, as not to show my figure. Also, the long sleeves, only showing my hands."

At the mentioning of the way she's dressed, Devon takes a moment to actually examine her, sad part is, she's right, but being the man he is, he just chalked it up to her liking to dress like a tomboy. "So... Where does this leave us?" Devon asks. "Do you want the truth?" She said, with a neutral expression on her face.

"To be honest...no, but I might as well live in reality, so, yeah, tell me the truth."

"Well, the truth is, it all depends on you."

"How's that?"

"With me being Muslim, there are certain things I just can't tolerate, nor am I." She said, a firmness in her voice that tells

236

Devan there is no room for compromise. "So, to be truthfully honest. If you're not going to revert to Islam. We can only be friends."

"So, you can't marry a Christian?"

"No. I'm not a man."

"You're not a man?"

"Yeah. It's permissible for a man. His job is to educate the woman, but you're not Muslim, nor studying the Quran and Sunnah... How can you equip me with the knowledge to properly implement my way of life? Also, I'm commanded to pray five times a day, a fast in the month of Ramadan, and I disagree with most of your way of life. How would that work?" She finishes, with a renowned sense of confidence she's yet to experience. For its one thing to say the words around Hamzah, but to do so with a surety that what she is standing on is the truth, is a totally different feeling.

The food gets cold as the silence between the two of them thickens like gravy sitting on the stove for too long. Devon contemplates what his mind is saying and what his heart is feeling.

If he said he doesn't have strong feelings for the woman sitting across from him, he would be lying. Yet to say he's ready to change his entire way of life for her is something of a totally different nature.

His thoughts are cut short when Consuela says, "It's time for Salat, well almost. Would you mind taking me to the Mosque?"

"Naw...not at all." Devon starts gathering his food, readying himself to leave.

On the way to the Mosque located on St. John's Bluff Blvd, Consuela is quiet, focusing totally on the coming Salat. Upon arrival, the Mu-ezzan has started the Alhan, the call to prayer.

237

Devon's heart is grasped by the firm melodic words sailing from the man's mouth as he chants.

"Allahu Akber! Allahu Akber!... Allaah huu Akbar... Allaahhuu Akbar." (God is great! God is great!)

Devon listens as the rest of the Adhan is finished and the Ryama is called. He watches as Consuela goes through the motions of the Salar, marveling at the unity the congregation of worshipers has. Each person bowing and standing in complete unison.

As Consuela approaches him afterwards, to him it seems as if a new calm has ascended over her. It's as if her face has a glow to it that wasn't present before. Looking into the windows to her soul, he can see the inner peace that shines within. "You look...calm."

"That is one of the reasons I became Muslim. The inner peace I feel after I prostrate before my Lord is one I can't find anywhere else. I found out why Hamzah is as calm as he is...

Why does it take so much anger to Him... And why He's the man He is." She walks out to the car.

On the ride home, the sounds of Drake rapping about wanting to be successful fill the car, but Devan's mind isn't on the music, yet on the woman sitting next to him. The future he may or may not have with her.

Once he drops Consuela off, he heads home to his three-bedroom house located in Orange Park, his cellphone ringing a tone he's all too familiar with. "Are you alone?" A deep voice questions, masked with a device designed to alter the caller's original voice.

"Yeah." he sighs. "Anything new?"

"She's taken her Shadah."

"Good, very good. Soon, she'll be of more help to us."

"Yeah," he says in an irritated tone.

"Is there something wrong Alex?"

"Hmmf." He sighs, "I don't think her or Hamzah have anything to do with the cell." He said, speaking of Hezbollah, a terrorist cell Alex Wright, A.K.A Devan, a 25-year-old military operative has been assigned to infiltrate. This being his first assignment, he was picked due to his boy-ish looks, giving him the ability to look younger than most operative, yet now that he's in the field, a problem has risen...Consuela and Islam.

First, his love for Consuela is starting to overshadow his perception and learning of Islam as it revealed, not the way it's being taught and interpreted by extremists. He's starting to see that Muslims have been trained to hunt and the ones he's in contact with, are two different groups.

"Well, Alex." The mechanic voice said. "It's not your job to make that assessment. Your job is to find the evidence."

"And if none exist?"

"Then neither do we, and neither do your subjects."

Chapter 19

It's a sunny day out as Neek sits in his apartment on Arlington Expressway in Oakhill. As sunny as it is outside, his mood is as dark as a cloudy night when the moon is covered.

Sitting on his leather sofa, the soft off-white color does nothing to listen to his mood. All he can think about is the feeling of betrayal that courses through his entire being, over the thought of Murder replacing him with Young.
The more he thinks about how merciless Murder was when giving him the news, the more his blood boils...
"Neek. What it is?" Murder said after a brief knock on the door of his hospital room.

"Yeah. What it is?" He replies, still bitter from the gunshot wound he was forced to endure. But being he was slipping; he somewhat understands Murder's stance.
"Listen." Murder said, pulling a chair up to Neek's bed. "Once you get out of this bed, you're going to be up under Young." He deadpans.

"What?" Neek tries to raise himself out of the bed as anger instantly starts to shoot to the surface. "Listen brah, I ain't bout to be up under a nigga younger than me!"
"Mm hmm." Murder sighs. "That is where you are totally wrong. First, you're acting as if you have some say in the matter, and that is where you fucked up!" Murder pauses, seeing the anger in Neek's eyes. "And to be honest, this situation reinforces my intention. All this anger!" He waves his hand in Neek's direction. "You have yet to separate your emotions from this business. Here it is, you fucked up and expect me to let it slide, don't you? Now, why is that? Because you are on some emotional shit that is clouding

240

your perception of the truth. In this game, ain't no room for fuck ups. If I have to clean up your mess, I might as well do the job myself. And brah, I'm a boss. I don't do janitorial work!" states Murder, causing Neek's anger to rise even more. Mainly because of the calm manner in which Murder is using and not at the words he knows are true.

Settling back, he tried to compose himself as Murder continues.

"What you understand Neck, is this dope game is a chessboard. Each and every move matters. What are the most important pieces on the board?" He shakes his head in disgust as Neck shrugs his shoulders. "The pawns. Why? Because each one of them has the potential to become a major piece. Of course in a chess sense, all pawns should aspire to become queens. We, well, I know the queens have a free range of movement, and you ain't even a queen. You're more of a knight or a bishop. My queen is Block, so it ain't shit to sacrifice you when one of my pawns can become a knight or a bishop later on in the game. Maybe." Murder smirks. "But all that emotional shit you on, gots to go. You let your lower desires put you in a position to take a loss and I ain't into losing. It's bad for the image." He smiles. "So, you can either work for Young or you don't, but realize that you doing you, means I must question your actions. And as much as I like you, I'm like the Duval County court system. You can be found guilty due to reasonable doubt." Murder finishes, calmly departing the room before Neek can respond, which silently informs him there is no room for discussion. Sitting on his sofa, Neek ponders Murder's words. Truth be told, he knows in his heart that Murder was right, but his sense of pride overshadows his ability to openly admit to the obvious truth.

Slowly, he stands up, stretching. The effects of the gunshots still prohibit his range of movement. Walking to his minibar filled with various liquors, he starts to attempt to formulate a plan for revenge, when his phone rings. "Yo!" he answers. "What it is Neek?" A voice said in response.

"Who is this?"

"Well my boy, let's just say...an enemy of your enemy, trying to be your friend."

"Listen brah! I don't know what the streets told you, but I ain't got no enemies!" Neek tries to place the voice.

"Come on now Neek! I saw the hurt on your face when I took you to the hospital..."

"Block!"

"Yep."

"How can you be the enemy of my enemy, when my enemy is your childhood friend?"

"Easy my nigga. Even the shadow at some point in the day is bigger than the man. It's my time to be bigger than the man." "How come?" Neek said, still suspicious.

"It's time. Murder has been in power too long. It's time he falls." Block pauses. "You in?"

Neek holds the phone for about a minute as Block patiently waits for an answer. After careful consideration, "I'm in. What do you have in mind?"

"That's what it do." And Neek can practically hear Block smile through the phone. "Let's just say, it's time we both get what is long overdue for us."

Hunter sits in front of his laptop examining the software system he personally designed. As he studies the chessboard in front of him, a game that only he knows he is playing, he somewhat smiles inwardly.

One of the main characteristics he loves about himself is his ability to remember any and everything he encounters in life, down to the most minute detail. Once when he was about it with a friend, he was informed he has a specific condition, he just never looked it up.

"My, my...Honey, you're borderline obsessed with this chess game of yours." The hands of an Arab female follow the angelic voice that spoke those words.

Looking at the initials AM on the board, with the Q on top, signifying that those initials are a queen. Hunter responds,

"My queen Amina...to say I am obsessed with this game would more than be an understatement, my dear." "But... Why?" Amina asks as she comes into his view, her medium-brown eyes outlined in emerald green, looking almost perfect with her sun-blasted skin, luscious lips, medium-sized nose, and dark black hair.

Hunter almost wants to rip her clothes off as he examines her slim waist, teardrop rear, and thick thighs. Sometimes, he finds it hard to believe she really, really loves him the way she does.

Their chance meeting wasn't one he thought would end in her wanting to see him again, yet the reason he murdered the man that claimed to be her husband was the fact that he was transgressing the limit of Shari'ah by beating Amina as if she was a grown man instead of the beautiful creation of Allah that she is.

But, even though he was defending her honor, the moment her husband's brains and skull splattered like a bucket of water, Hunter would've fully understood if she never wanted to see him again. Yet the next day, she somehow showed up at his hotel door.

"Well my jewel," Hunter pulls her close to him, "In the Quran, Allah the Exalted says: "He created Jinn and Mankind to only worship Him" ... As you obviously know." He smiles, "of course, I'm not, nor can ever be Allah, yet He has endowed me with the intellect to control the men and women in my life, by always being steps ahead of them... So, that is what this game is about."

"Really." She grabs the laptop, looking at the chessboard, "If so... What part in this game of yours do I play?"

At her question, Hunter's smile widens, "That my eternity is the most important part of the game, yet." He holds his finger up, "This entire story has yet to unfold, so to tell you the part you're going to play, would only spoil the end, and this story is many books long. Spanning many lives."

***

A month later, Hamzah sits in his house, on the phone with Consuela as she checks in, informing him she's going to stay the night at a friend of her's house. "Listen Connie" he smiles into the phone, "You do not have to check in with me."

"Yes, I do, you're my Wali," Consuela responds, confirming that Islamically, Hamzah is her protector, father, etc...

"Since when?"

"Since my declaration."

"I... I... I mean." Hamzah stutters. Yes, he does see Consuela as his daughter in a sense, but to hear her say those words, touches his heart.

"Listen Hamzah, truth be told, you're the closest thing to a father figure I've had in my entire life, so it is what it is. I love you. As-salamu Alaykum."

"As-salamu Alaykum." He hangs the phone up, allowing their conversation to really soak into his mind.

Since Hamzah left the army, he only had himself to live for. Therefore it was easy to live life as a contract killer. Because at the end of the day, if he never came home, nobody would miss him. Now Consuela has changed all of that. There was someone that would be affected by his death. Someone would miss him. So now his exit from that life is a must.

"Who the fuck are you, and what the fuck are you doing in my house?" Hamzah said through gritted teeth at the sight of a small Mexican man in the mirror above his fireplace.

"No, how did I get in!" The male smiles.

"Doesn't matter. Answer my questions."

"The name is El Mole...and I'm here because I was paid to be here."

"Paid? Paid for what?"

"Aw...come on now Hamzah." El Mole says.

"Well, you had better give them their money back!" Hamzah laughs.

"Give the money back...why?" El Mole places his hands in his pockets, leaning on the inside of the door.

"Because." Hamzah stands up. "I finally have a reason to really stay on this earth, so..." Hamzah cracks his fingers.

"You can give them their money back or leave here in a bag."

"A bag. Nobody bag?"

"Hell no! Listen, Mole, I don't call the authorities, I'll just stuff your little ass in a bag and dump you in the trash!"

"Wow! You sound so confident!" El Mole stands upright.

"Only one way to find out." Hamzah walks towards him. As he does, he notices El Mole doesn't so much as flinch. This instance alerts him. One of the key lessons any professional fighter learns is in the midst of battle, the calm one usually wins.

Once in range, as a test, Hamzah shoots a swift straight at him and isn't shocked as El Mole easily sidesteps the strike. Blocking with his left hand, placing himself outside of the punch, grasping Hamzah's wrist with a swan fist, attempting to strike his knee with a low side thrust that Hamzah counters by bending his right knee, sweeping with his left leg, which El Mole dodges by jumping backwards out of range. "Did you really think that was going to work?" El Mole smiles.

"Oh, hell no, just had to find out what I'm up against."

"Now you know. My turn!" El Mole said, rushing Hamzah with a swift combination of overhands, jabs, uppercuts, and crosses.

As Hamzah easily blocks the strikes, he does so with a laugh, not even attempting to counter with a strike. El Mole continues his onslaught of strikes, with kicks, knees, elbows, the whole while getting frustrated as Hamzah weaves, sidesteps, blocks, and parries all his strikes as if he's a white belt in Shotokan.

"You must be kidding!" Hamzah sits on the back of his chair laughing as El mole stands across the room panting from exhausting himself. "I tell you what," Hamzah says, walking to the small fridge in the room, opening it, tossing El Mole a bottle of Aquafina. "The one thing I must admit, you're pretty damn good, just not good enough to beat me. So, I'm going to allow you to leave my house with your life...or you can die right this minute." Hamzah said, turning around from closing the fridge, smiling. "Great choice!" He smiles, finding El Mole gone.

***

El Mole escapes to his Dodge Challenger, opening the driverside door, settling in.

"Tsk! Tsk! Tsk!" A voice says from the backseat.

At the sound of the intruder's voice, a gun instantly appears in El Mole's hand as he places it inches from Hunter's face. "Hey!" Hunter throws his hands up. "I'm not the enemy! I just saw your last bout and I must say, you really underestimated your opponent."

"Senor...you have sixty seconds, ten seconds ago to tell me why you are here." El Mole says without an ounce of humor in his voice.

"Oh! Well that is easy." responds Hunter, "How do you feel about the game of chess?" He smiles. ***

Truth be told, ever since me and Si have been back in the Ville, things have taken a turn for the better. I guess part of that lies in the fact that I've finally realized that the only thing stopping me from loving Si is me.

Now, I'm not saying that I'm a changed man, not by a long shot. But in order to really change, one must start the process. To do that, you gotta keep it one hundred with yourself. For me, the truth of the matter is...I ain't shit! Yeah, that really is what it comes down to. The entire time I thought I was being a super dad to my angel. I was really missing almost all of her life. To put it simply, it's like I was in prison doing a long bid, telling myself I was being a father. Yeah, I am her father, but on those nights she needed me to chase away the boogie man, I might as well have been in an eight-by-ten cell. At least then I would've had a better excuse, ya feel me?

Time my niggas. That's the key. That's the most important thing any father can give to their loved ones...time. Time to love you. Time to understand how much you really love them. Time to build memories. Most importantly, time allows you to be a part of those memories. So far, my father's behind the gates. You spend a lot of time being a ghost in the picture, once you can be a part of the polaroid. Try not just doing so on Saturdays and Sundays when the crackers call your name. Do it on Saturdays and Sundays, also Monday through Friday when your angels open their eyes my nigga. The streets are a popular T.V. show. If you can't catch the new episodes, you can always catch the re-runs, ya feel me?

"Have you found Tivia yet so we can find out who destroyed the studio?" Sienna asked me, gliding to the bedroom.

"That's the crazy part is I can't even come close to even knowing where she was last, let alone finding her now."

"Don't you think that is strange?" She puts her hair in a ponytail, then I notice she has on one of her many jogging suits.

"Where are you going?"

"Where does it look like? Jogging!"

"Jogging?" I respond, "Si, this is not the time to just be running around the neighborhood. Yeah." I hold my hands up, "Things have been relatively quiet, but we can't slip."

"True, very true." She smiles, holding her shirt up revealing the silenced .22 in the waist holster under her shirt. "I'm not wearing loose clothing for nothing."

"Yeah, but still... I'm coming with you." I push up off the bead, getting dressed. "Plus I need the exercise."

Moments later, I find that the brisk jog was a need. As the air flows into my lungs, and blood starts circulating, the small distance we thought we were going to run turns out to be us jogging from our neighborhood in Mandarin, all the way to a small plaza a couple of miles away.

Once there, we decide to grab us a foot-long sub and split it. "Damn bae!" I said around a mouth full of chips. "I ain't gone lie!... I really needed that lil bit of exercise."

"Oh! What are you saying I don't work you out enough?" She smiles mischievously.

"What? If anything, I be working that ass out!" I mimic her bending her, causing her to laugh.

"You know bae." I grab her hand. "I'm not going to lie to you, in the last couple of months, I finally realize that you are a very important part of my life, and truth be told, I owe you a lot. I plan to spend the rest of my life making it up to you."

"Neiros." She says. Tears in her eyes. "Do you know how long I've been waiting to hear you say that?"

"Yeah I do, but..." I pause, trying to find the right words. "I'm not going to make any promises to be this perfect man. I'd be lying if I said I am, but I do understand that I have a problem.

I'm a sex addict, so please, bear with me."

"Baby." She exhales. "Yes, your cheating has been a major problem, but..." She holds both of my hands. "you're not being there is more of a problem than anything. Do you think I expect you to be perfect? No. Did I think you were going to be totally faithful to me? No. This is why. Do you remember what I did while you were in prison?"

"Yeah..." I nod my head. "You were a waitress."

"Yes, well one time I had this older black couple. They were there to celebrate their twentieth anniversary. I asked them what was their secret. How did they stay together for so long? Well, the man pointed at the woman who said, I let him be a man. Once he saw that I wasn't going anywhere,

249

all the cheating and bullshit stopped. So, baby, I'm not telling you it's okay to cheat on me, but as long as you come home to me and our daughter...I'm not going nowhere."

"Damn girl, I love you!" I embrace my wife. This woman that I truly do not deserve, "Damn, it's gotten quiet!" I said, noticing that not one person in the small restaurant is even whispering.

Clap! Clap! Clap! "It's about damn time you notice." Says a blond-haired female in a Swiss accent, "But, by any means, please, finish having your moment." She extends her arms at us, "It's quite touching. Wouldn't you say mum?"

"Not really Day." Another blond bombshell replies, yet to say she looks like her daughter's mother, would be almost crazy, being she looks just as young as Day does.

"Well, that's why you're Night and I'm Day, mum."

"Alright, enough with the bullshit! Why are you here?" My wife demands, and with a wave of the hand, Night brings to our attention that not only is the place totally empty, but all of the staff is dead.

No need for any further prompting, me and Sienna almost simultaneously flip the table, pulling our firearms just as the Switzerland duo open fire.

The sound of the silenced pistols is akin to very big bees buzzing around the room. But unlike the movies, silencers do not stay silent for the entire clip. So just as Night and Day start to replace theirs, I and Sienna dash out the front door into the blinding Sun.

Quickly, we find a van to hide behind when my phone rings. "Jizzle!"

"Yo! Jizzle some Kuffar just tried to kill me, but he wasn't that good." laughs Hamzah.

"Well Hamzah, some Kuffars are trying to kill me now, and these bitches are pretty damn good!" I reply, just as the front window of the van shatters, forcing me and Sienna to leave the cover of the van, returning fire at the duo.

"Do you need me?"

"No! No, we got this…just meet me at the spot tomorrow." I hang the phone up while pushing this young dude out the way as he's about to get into his car.

Pointing the gun at him, I demand he gives me the keys.

"Yo, yo bro!" He yells with his hands up. "If you need a ride I got you, bro!"

At first, I'm totally shocked this man would say that but now isn't the time. Because I see Night and Day heading across the parking lot, hands on their pistols until their shirts.

"Alright!

Alright!' He moves over as Sienna gets in the back seat.

"Let's go!"

"No problem man!" The man jumps behind the wheel.

As I make our getaway, I smile at Night and Day, as they calmly stare at me returning my smile.

Chapter 20

Alex Wright listens as Hamzah talks about the Kuffar trying to kill him, and a deep sinking feeling enters his chest. As much as his heart is telling him that both Hamzah and Connie aren't the terrorists that he has trained to believe they are, the words coming out of Hamzah's mouth only confirm what he has been taught.

"Devon!" Hamzah opens the door with a smile. "What are you doing here?"

"Well." Devon composes himself. "I've been thinking... I really love Connie, but I understand that I and her can't be together until I take my Shahadah."

"Whoa! Whoa! Whoa!" Hamzah starts waving his hands, "Devon, there is no compulsion in religion."

"Okay."

"Well, I will not allow you to take your Shahadah for any other reason than that you are doing so for the sake of Allah only. Not for Connie and me."

"Oh of course not." Devon feels he's found his way in. "Listen Hamzah, I'm for the cause."

"The cause?" Hamzah tilts his head.

"Yeah, ever since I've been around you and Connie, I finally understand how the Kuffar are trying to destroy the beauty that is Islam."

"Kuffar... the beauty that is Islam?"

"Yeah. Isn't that what you were talking about just now on the phone."

"What? Hell naw!" Hamzah laughs, "Devon, I'm not some sort of Jihadist. I was just using that term loosely man. Listen, the root of the word Kuffaar is Kafara, which means to conceal. How can you or anybody else conceal something that you have no knowledge of? Now, you are in the state of Kafir. A state of disbelief, but a Kafir... no."

252

"But the phone call..." Devon said, confused.

"Hmm." Hamzah sighs, "Devon, how much can I trust you?"

"Honestly Hamzah...I don't know."

Taken aback by his answer, Hamzah responds, "Granted, I'm not exactly sure what that means, but I've seen the love you have for Connie, and I truly believe unless you must, you wouldn't hurt her."

"Never."

"Well, I'm a hitman."

"What? That's it? You're not a terrorist!"

"What? Fuck no! Devon, the only Jihad I'm undergoing is the education of the Muslim man. Granted, these Muslims on the Hagg overseas are still my brothers. They transgress the limits of the Shari'ah, but I'm going to also say Allahu A'lam, for I don't know their struggle and what could be wrong."

"Wow!" Devon whips his head, "Man, that just took a big burden off my shoulders!"

"I'm lost." Questions Hamzah.

"Trust me, it's nothing, but I thought you were a Jihadist trying to recruit Connie for domestic terrorism."

The expression on Hamzah's face turns into a block of stone, making it hard for Devon to read exactly what's on his mind. "Hamzah...you good?" He asks, backing up a little.

"The question is, are you good?" responds Hamzah, face still a statue.

"I... I mean yeah... Why wouldn't I be?"

"Listen, Devan, I know there is something you're keeping from me, and my gut instinct tells me that it's very important. So..." He sighs, "What is it?"

At that moment, Devon knows he is in between a rock and a hard place. He can't tell Hamzah the truth because he knows his boss will more than likely have him eliminated, but lying to Hamzah doesn't seem to be the route out of this situation as well.

"Listen" he starts, "Hamzah, I can't really tell you the truth."

"Why?" Hamzah cocks his head to the side.

"Because not only can me and you be killed by knowing it., more than likely, so will Connie."

"Damn." sighs Hamzah, "Devon, here's the situation... I can't let you continue to come around Connie with the thought of her being... Hold on." Hamzah said, answering his phone.

"As-salamu Alaykum!" El Mole says, "I hope all is well after our last meeting."

"You again." Hamzah immediately recognizes the voice. "What do you want?"

"Wrong question."

"Really? So the right one would be?"

"Who... Do... I... Have?" El Mole said, allowing silence to deepen the impact of his words.

"Where is Connie?" Hamzah places his hand over the phone asking Devon, who immediately flees the room in search of her.

"Listen, listen, listen!" El Mole says, "I've got the bitch...and don't say the whole, if you touch one hair on her head, thing. That's so nineteen-eighties!"

"You know I'm going to kill you right?" Hamzah says, laughter in his voice, which is the total opposite of the response El Mole expected.

"Oh! You find this situation funny, huh?" El Mole responds and Hamzah can feel the smile in his voice.

"Not really," says Hamzah. "The thing is this...in life, you have two types of killers. The first is motivated by money. You see him," Hamzah laughs. "He has two types of endings. The first. He ends up being emotionally detached by associating his murders with only being a job. A thing

254

that must be done to get the money he needs to survive. In the next ending, he becomes tormented by the sight of death every day until he either has to quit or find a way to end his life."

"That's great, but you said there are two types of killers?" questions El Mole.

"Yes. The reason I laugh, 'm the second type of killer. The money is only secondary to the thrill of murder. You see, having to find even more ways to murder...maim...torture..." Hamzah pauses, "gives me more pleasure than any amount of money ever could."

"Really, and which one do you think I am?"

"It really doesn't matter, does a lion even contemplate what type of animal it has to fight?" Hamzah chuckles, "The thing is, I put this side of me to rest. Yet, you've awakened it. So, if you ain't ready to die...Connie better be home soon. Real soon."

"Ha! Ha!" El mole bursts into a fit of laughter. "You really think highly of yourself! I mean..."

"What the fuck?" yells El Mole, "This muthafucka!" He looks at his cell phone upon realizing that Hamzah had hung up after his statement. "Well..." He turns to look at Consuela, "I guess he's really upset..." He smiles, "Oh well, it's your life on the line." He laughs, then frowns. "Why are you smiling?" "Oh me?" Connie responds. "The Prophet Muhammad once told a young boy, "Just know, If the whole world came together to hurt you, they could only hurt as much as Allah has decreed, and if the whole world came together to benefit you, they can only benefit you as much as Allah has decreed."

"O.K."

"Well, you can only do what was been already decreed. If that's death, Al-Hamidullah. Also, I know Hamzah."

"So?"

"He won't rest until he makes sure that you are in the Hellfire!"

***

Standing outside Flow looks around at the sight of money being made. Since he put things in motion, the cash has been flowing in at a constant pace. He stays in constant contact with Smoke and granted C.J. isn't following his lifestyle choices, he still stays in contact with Flow.

In his mind, he ponders that face. Flow understands exactly what being a real friend is about. Most niggas are only down with you if you're doing the things, they feel are right. Yet a real friend, he is going to be by your side despite the fact the two of you are on different pages. He guesses that is because C.J. once told him "I don't fuck with it because of what you do, but who you are."

"Yo! Flow! What's good? Amor de Rey!" yells Smash, walking across the street.

"Amor de Rey!" greets Flow, taking the young soldier in. The thing he admires about Smash is his loyalty. The young hustler is ferociously loyal, a quality not too prevalent in the youth these days.

"Yo! Listen, the paper at the spot. What's good with the work?"

"The same spot," replies Flow, just as a bullet pings of the brownstone behind him, alerting him that someone is shooting at him. "Oh shit!... Guard up Smash!"

"I'm on it homey!" responds Smash, turning around, pulling out two black 9mm.

"Yeah, son!" He yells, walking toward the three men letting the nines sing a murderous song. "Yeah, son! Shit real around here!"

Flow looks on as three men take cover, not expecting the young soldier to respond. "Amor de Rey!" yells Smash, whistling.

Instantly, two more young soldiers no more than fourteen or fifteen years of age emerge from around the corner, pistols in hand, bullets flying from them like missiles from a fighter jet, fire lighting the almost dark evening up like the Fourth of July has come early.

Standing, Flow laughs to himself as three men flee the scene, making Usain Bolt look slow.

"Chill my niggas!" yells Smash, "Yo homey, you good?" he turns to Flow.

"Yeah, lil soulja." Flow daps him up, "What do you think that was about?"

"Well homey," Smash puts his pistols away, "A lot of niggas been in their feelings about how we moving, ya feel me?"

"Yeah." Flow puts his unused pistol away.

"Yeah, but that shit ain't a problem. I got the security shit on lock."

"True, but we gotta make a statement…so find out who in their feelings."

"Alright, then what?"

"We gone give them something to cry about."

"I'm on it. Amor de Rey." Smash turns and leaves just as Flow's phone rings.

"Yo!"

"I see you trying to get ya weight up." A familiar voice from the past says.

"My weight been up homey."

"Yeah, you ran last time. What you plan on doing this time?"

"I ain't run homey. Just out of dodge. This time, I'm going to find out who you are and put an end to this shadow man shit." "Well, I'm a put the guessing game to an end…"

From across the street, a car door opens and sends Flow instantly into the past, as his father emerges from the vehicle in an all-white Armani suit, an evil grin painted on his face.

Flow immediately draws his pistol only to hear the cocking of a gun from behind, coming from the steps of the brownstone. Flow eases the pistol down to his side.

"Thought you'd see it my way." His father grins, the spiderweb scar on his face given to him by his only son giving the grin an eerie look.

"This how you gone play it?" asks Flow.

"Never Son…"

"Don't call me your fucking son!" Flow sneers.

"I'll call you whatever the fuck I want son!" snaps his father. "But this is just a family courtesy. Trust me, the next time I run down on you, it ain't gone be pretty."

"Yeah." Flow smiles, "The one thing you forgot," he said, waving his hand, and instantly a shot comes from a window of a brownstone across the street, dropping the man behind him as he steps forward, placing his pistol against the scar on his face. "I ain't fifteen anymore…so I'm always ready. Since you gave me a family courtesy…I'll give you one." He points to the car his father came out of. "But just know the next time you see my face… You'll be dead."

***

Sitting in my new office chair inside of my new headquarters for Reality Records, me and Hamzah watched the video of Hunter murdering Shi'ama. The only thing I can think about is the recent turn of events that have led up to this moment. Throughout my life, I always maintained that I have utter control over all things that have taken place, but even the name of my record label has been controlled by Hunter. When I was young, he told me "Neiros, you must understand that the concept of reality is only relevant to the mind in which contains it. You can decide what reality is for whoever decides to enter your form of reality. The truth is always based on two factors, the known and the unknown. What you decide to let people know decides what their perceived reality of you is, yet understand, this reality cannot be based on a lie. In order to maintain a lie, you'll have to invent other lies. Then you'll lose sight of your own reality. Now the question remains..."

At that moment is when it hits me. You see, Hunter's next words explain that in order to not become swept up into someone else's fake reality, you must master being a seeker of the unknown. You have to uncover the traces of the articles of that person's life that they don't want you to see. Hunter has done exactly that. He is a master of the unknown. The skeletons that people hide inside of their closets. He has a way of pulling them out, only for himself to examine. This entire time, I've always been under the impression that I was painting the perfect picture of a false reality. When in all actuality, I've been living in another one my entire life.

"So," I look at Hamzah once the video is done, "You see what we are dealing with?"

"Yeah." he sighs, and I can tell that it's more than just the video of Hunter that's bothering him.

"What's the problem?"

"To be truthful my brother," he leans up steepling his fingers while looking off into space. "Since you told me that I would earn all that money for completing that job, all I could think about is placing this life behind me, yet the shaitan always finds a way to pull me back." "Yeah," I answer, mostly as a way to allow him time to vent. Me personally, I am not a very religious man. Granted, I believe in God, but I'm one to practice religion.

Now Hamzah, he is really on his din, as they say in the Islamic world. Everything revolves around Islam. His every decision, step, etc. He's one of the first Muslims I have met that has a very comprehensive understanding of why Islam is a way of life.

259

He once told me that most people have this crazy notion that the moment you utter a few words, you'll be this insanely upright, perfect person. But to believe that, not saying some people can't achieve it, would be neglecting the simple concept of human nature.

For most people, life is a rollercoaster ride of ups and downs. Today, your quantity of faith may be high, tomorrow, not so much. The wisdom of Islam dictates that the quality of faith doesn't rise nor fall. You either believe or you don't, the only thing that can take you out of faith is that which has brought you in.

"Yeah." he continues. "I had this well thought out plan to be sitting at the feet of a shaykh in Morrocco by the end of the year, but..."

"But what?"

"He took Connie." He says, letting the reality of those words settle in. You see, between like-minded individuals, most of the time nothing has to be said in order for a statement to be made.

I've never met Consuela, only heard about her from Hamzah. That in itself says a lot. Usually, Hamzah has no problem with me meeting any female he meets. For him to not want Connie to meet me, tells me that he wanted to shield her from the lifestyle that I live.

Most people would take that as an insult. But in truth that's the reality of things, just because he acknowledges that and wants to protect her from being exposed to my wicked ways (and we can all agree they are wicked) doesn't diminish our friendship in any way. I totally understand, so with both of us being killers, I feel him. The person that has kidnapped that girl, is in for a world of hurt. "Yeah bro," I respond. "But you can always get back to that once this is done."

"Yeah, the problem is when. The one thing I know is I'm about to go off into the abyss, Jizzle. The monster is back. I feel it in my chest. That…that hunger for revenge. That, that…" He stutters, fingers cringing in front of his face, eyes void of that light that makes us all human. "That total satisfaction that can only come from seeing the life leave the body by the way of the eyes."

Watching Hamzah, I totally understand. Those feelings he is describing are like intoxicating liquor. The man's weakness, that man knows that Satan takes advantage of those that want to be that in which he cannot, and that is God.

For many, the feeling of total and utter domination of another soul is that closeness to being like the creator. The knowledge that you have a moment's control over the coming or going of another being, is almost as addictive as any known drug to man, but the comedown. Yeah, that's the muthafucka. The comedown comes from the moment you inflict severe injury to the body of a person, that should end their life, yet God shows you why you aren't Him. When he decides it's not that person's time. Then, you start the journey all addicts travel. The path to recreate a feeling that you know the end result of. "But" Hamzah snaps back, "Those are bridges that will have to be passed once I reach them. Now, it's time to be that monster."

"Let's go," I say, getting up and following Hamzah into the conference room across the hall.

Once inside, I look at my team. First, I take in my wife Sienna. I know she is prepared for the battle that is in front of us, but can I stand to take the chance to lose her. It's one thing to place myself in harm's way because that would leave her to fend for our daughter, but I know in my heart that Hunter wouldn't allow her to sit on the sideline.

Then there's Murder. Yeah, he's a real soulja, but is he ready for this pressure that Hunter is about to bring? Trust me, the next saga of this story is going to be a bloody one. Full of murder and mind games.

"Listen," I said as I walk towards the back of the conference room, grasping the back of the chair at the head of the table. "In life, you have soldiers, and you have warriors. The soldier is the one that follows orders, even if that means the odds of certain death are higher than they would be if he decided not to. The warrior lives by the rule of self-preservation. He will only follow those orders that make sense. If they do not make perfect sense, he will improvise in the name of survival..." I pause, knowing that what I'm about to ask of these people is nothing short of crazy. "I don't need soldiers for this battle. Truth be told, if you enter this battle as a soldier, you will not see the end of the war. Honestly, if I could leave you out of the situation I would. But the man we are about to go to war with, will not allow that to happen... Just so you know, everything you hold sacred...your loved ones, friends, are all at risk of getting murdered. In war, there are no innocents except kids."

"Yo Jizzle." interrupts Murder. "Brah, I ain't ever been a follower, nor am I about to fear any man on this Earth. If he's human, he can bleed...if he can bleed, he can..."

He is interrupted by the door to the conference room opening. In the doorway stands Tivia and Akema. The look in Tivia's eyes along with the tears that cascade down her beautiful face immediately tell me that the pistol in her hands is not there for good reasons.

"Tivia," I said, trying to play this situation by ear.

"Why Jizzle?"

"Why what Tivia?" I ask calmly, being sure to place my hand on my own pistol in the holsters under my arm.

"You know what!"

"Tivia. Actually, no, I don't have the slightest idea what you are talking about."

"You murdered my father!" she yells, lifting her pistols and aiming them my way, which immediately causes a domino effect as pistols appear in hands like Chris Angel's magic tricks.

"Akema?" I ask, tilting my head to the side.

"Death...I'm with Tivia."

"The whole play your position shit?"

"Yea...that was then, this is now. The veil has finally been lifted." She said, and that statement has more to it than she's willing to reveal at this moment, but now isn't the time. "Tivia." I turn my attention back to her, "I don't even know who your father is."

"Liar!" Her hands tense on the pistols.

"Tivia!" I say forcefully. "Look at this situation. There's no way you're going to make it out of here alive..." I motion to all the guns pointed at her. "Let's take a moment. Chill. Talk this out."

"Hmmf." She smiles and I realize at that moment, this is about to get ugly. "Jizzle...the point ain't to make it out alive. Just get your target."

The moment she finishes those words, the room erupts in a storm of gunfire. I swiftly let off shots, ducking behind the chair in an attempt to dodge the bullets coming my way.

From behind the chair, I return fire to Akema, who expertly peppers the room with shots from the AR-15 in her hands. Hamzah is forced to duck behind the chair in front of him, which is a disadvantage from the array of lead Akema lets lose.

I watch helplessly as Young is caught in the onslaught of a lead Akema sends at various targets. Alex tries to use the suppression fire technique taught to him in the military, but Akema is a real expert with this assault rifle.

She covers Tivia as she exits the room. Backing out behind her, I immediately rise up to give chase. "Jizzle!" I hear Hamzah yell my way. "I gotta catch these bitches!" I said through gritted teeth.

"Jizzle... Si!"

The words out of his mouth stopped me cold. Looking his way, Tivia's words down on me. Her target was never me. That would not allow me to feel the pain that she was feeling. But to kill Si. "No, no, no, no!" My mouth says on autopilot. I swiftly run to Sienna's side, tears streaming down my face. "Somebody call an ambulance! Please!" I cradle my wife to my chest. "Come on Si! Not now! Come on bae!"

"Ne... Neiros..." She says weakly, blood on her lips. "You gone kill me if you keep squeezing me!" she tries to smile. "Listen" I smile, "Don't you die on me. You die on me, I'm a kill you. You hear me? You die on me...I'm a kill you!" "Alright Ike." she smiles, and that smile melts my heart. No matter how much bullshit I talk, I can't live without this woman. This is my Eve. "Bae, where are you hit?" "Nigga! I don't know! Just get me to the hospital!" She playfully punches me on the chest just as the paramedics rush into the room.

***

Later that night, after answering a thousand questions the detectives asked me knowing damn well, I wasn't going to answer them, I sit in the hospital with Sienna, who is going to survive a bullet to the mid-section. Wish I could say the same for Young. The H.R. bullets were not as nice as the 9mm bullets that hit Si.

Nobody was able to catch Tivia and Akema. So, I sent the team home on high alert. I was exhausted with blood still on my clothes until Hamzah brought me some more, I almost hesitate as the door opens and Hunter walks in with a coat over his hand concealing the silenced pistol.

"Ah! My prodigy." He says with a smile on his face. "Now, you can go for the pistol you have close by and..." He waves the pistol in his hand.

"Alright." I said resigned. "If this is how it's going to end...let's do it."

"Ha, ha, ha!" he laughs. "Do you really think I would've gone through all that I have, just to do something I could've done from the beginning?" His head drops. "Really."

"Then what is this?"

"When you were a kid, was it more fun to play by yourself or with an opponent?... Of course, you're not going to answer that, but I can continue this game with you in the dark."

"So this is all a game to you!" I shout, pointing at Sienna.

"Whoa! Temper, temper! Too much emotion. But yes, despite your emotional attachment to shit I could give two fucks about...I must entertain myself." And with that he pulls out a piece of paper, tossing it on the floor, and just as silently as he appeared, he disappeared.

I get out of my chair, picking the piece of paper up. Looking at it with mixed emotions of disgust, hatred, and horror, on the piece of paper is an actual chessboard. Hunter is sick. This man truly has no regard for human life, it's really only entertainment.

"Yo! Jizzle you good?" Murder said, rushing into the room, gun drawn.

"Yeah...I'm good." I stare at the paper.

"Here's your clothes." Hamzah hands me a clean change of clothes.

"Jizzle, you sure you good?" Murder questions again.

"Yeah, homie! Why you keep asking?"

"Look in the hallway."

The moment I walk into the hallway, my face loses all of its blood. The sight of the entire late-night shift staff murdered in cold blood greets me. The night nurse lies on the counter face first, her brains all over the counter.

The security detail assigned to this floor lay slumped against the wall. The scream from another nurse pierces the silence that brings us out of our small foreign world. "Damn." Murder says, "Hunter did this?" "Yeah Murder."
"This is what we gotta be…"
Murder is interrupted as a swarm of officers file of the elevator, headed our way. "Bout time," I say.
"Mr. Neiros Simmons." The first officer says.
"That's me."
"Sir, you're under arrest for the murder of Alonzo Menez."
The moment he says that my phone alerts me of a new message. Pulling it up, it's Hunter and it says," The game has begun. Be prepared."

To be continued…

About the Author

David Ruffin was born and raised in Fort Myers, Florida in a loving family in the rough part of Fort Myers. The Michigan Court apartment 4224 Michigan Court Apt. #209 is better known as the Hood. He is well known in the city streets of Fort Myers.

Mr. Ruffin learned the love and gift of cooking food at a very early age from his grandparents and took lots of trips to Alabama. He also boxed at an early age but gave it up to play Football.

Life wasn't always great for the Author, in and out of trouble in the 90's and 2000. Thankfully, he changed his life for the better and still tries hard to keep a smile on his face after being illegally pulled over and beaten by a Fort Myers Police Department Officer on December 3, 2018.

I truly appreciate and thank the witnesses that called the police on the police when I was getting kicked, punched multiple times, tased multiple times, choked while handcuffed and Screaming I Can't Breathe as well, I was punched in the chest multiple times in the backseat of the police vehicle.

I never thought I'll be a victim of Police Brutality! Sign My petition at change.org for David Ruffin.

Made in the USA
Columbia, SC
26 November 2022

72128983R00150